Collection of Dreams

Derek Allen

This is a work of fiction. Names and characters are the product of the author's imagination and any resemblance to actual persons, living or dead, is entirely coincidental.

ISBN 978-1-912964-61-1 (Paperback)

www.cranthorpemillner.com

Published by Cranthorpe Millner Publishers (2020)

About the Author

After careers in the retail and transport industries, as a mature student Derek Allen came late into academia. Beginning with a history-based honours degree at what was then Worcester College of Higher education, he stayed at Worcester to complete a Masters before embarking on a doctorate centring on Independent Radio in the West Midlands. Graduating in 2011 with his thesis Independent Local Radio (ILR) in the West Midlands, 1972-1984, Derek was the first doctorate to be awarded by the University of Worcester (until then doctorates were evaluated by Coventry University).

Now working part time in retail while writing primarily fiction, Derek still has a keen interest in political and media history.

About the Author

Acknowledgements

What began with a short story, tentatively entitled *The Journey*, which later became *The Girl with the White T-shirt*, *Collection of Dreams* has been the result of ideas explored, then rejected, drafts written, modified, then put aside in favour of much better efforts. In all, it has a long, interesting, though at times agonising road. But enjoyable. So here we are, the final article, all done, dusted and ready for the reading world.

There are a lot of people who I would like to thank in making all this possible. Firstly, and importantly, Kirsty and her team at Cranthorpe Millner for having faith in this fledgling writer and taking him on board. Then editing (and in places improving), and after a couple of proofs presenting this final article.

Before all this came the actual writing. In part, thanks must therefore go to friends and colleagues for their encouraging comments after reading through what were early and basic drafts. Then, when the finished article was ready for releasing to wider world, special thanks must go to Karol and Debz for their critical reviews and helpful comments.

Finally, thank you, the reader, for selecting my first attempt at fictional writing.

Hope you enjoy!

Contents

The Girl with the White T-shirt

Wednesday the ninth of May 2007, six-fifteen p.m. He had been at work since seven that morning, and he was exhausted. The seminar presentation had taken much longer than anticipated; he had not realised how many people would be interested in the social history of the London Underground. That question and answer session had taken forever! Still, it was nice to know his months of painstaking research and writing had finally paid off, and he was encouraged by how many people had promised to buy his forthcoming book. He had worked at the University for just over twenty years, making his way up the ranks to become Head of History, as well as a senior research fellow and Chair of the Examiner's Board. It was mostly because of the latter that he was exhausted; the end of the second semester was always the busiest time of the academic year, what with examinations to organise, grades for the whole university to be finalised...and two history modules worth of exam papers to mark.

But right now, his plan consisted of going home and forgetting everything, at least until tomorrow. After all, it would not be long until the summer break, and then he could concentrate on finishing his book. There was not much left to do now that the final draft was with the publisher, just a few last-minute alterations. If he could get it finished at the start of the break, he might even be able to get away this year; find himself a cheap flight and hotel package or something. Holidays had been a rarity during the last few years, and he could really do with some relaxation time.

He considered where he might go as he put on his favourite summer jacket. It had seen better days, and the once cream colour that had so perfectly complemented the dark hair of his youth now matched his greyness. He was getting too old for all this, too old to be carrying on with this daily grind.

The jacket was almost as old as the battered briefcase he carried with him every day. He had bought it years ago, to celebrate his new teaching job at the University, and it had been with him ever since. In truth, by this point in his career, he was too frightened to go without it. He was superstitious enough to look on it as his lucky charm, despite what his more modern colleagues thought, with their swanky, wheeled cases. It was their loss. They had the space to take the job home with them, and felt compelled to do so, whereas for him, home was a place of rest.

Meetings, planning, filling in forms, more meetings, more forms to fill in...nowadays, he felt like a mere functionary amidst the bureaucracy the job had become. He reflected on this as he left work each evening, always making a conscious effort to look back at the Senate House where the University was based. He imagined himself as the character Winston Smith leaving the Ministry of Truth, in his favourite novel *Nineteen Eighty-Four*; an appropriate comparison, given that the Senate House had been requisitioned by the government to house the Ministry of Information during the Second World War, which Orwell had renamed the Ministry of Truth. Like Smith, he too led a lonely existence, having divorced his wife twelve years ago. He had since taken up residence in a small flat in Colindale, where he was now heading.

His usual route to the Tube was via Keppel, then Store Streets, to catch the Northern Line at Goodge Street on Tottenham Court Road. But as it was a nice evening, he decided to take a leisurely stroll and catch the Tube at Euston instead. Dodging the joggers and cyclists, who used Tavistock Square as a running circuit and a short cut to Bloomsbury, he lit a cigarette and ambled across the square, enjoying the tranquillity. It was a longer route, but it was a welcome alternative to his usual congested journey home, and there was the added bonus of an occasional glance at the sunbathers as they lounged on the grass, soaking up the evening sun. Looking at the women, most of them at least half his age, he could not help but wish they had been around when he was younger. Back then, women had been more conservative in the way they dressed, and sunbathing had been restricted to the beach; no one had sunbathed in the parks when he was a young man.

The peaceful respite ended when he reached Euston Road, where he could taste and smell the foul fumes rising from the rush hour traffic. In recent years, the air quality in London had grown steadily worse, and during the hot summer months it was guaranteed to be even more polluted. His ageing lungs, already silted up from years of smoking, did not appreciate the challenge.

He waited for the crossing signal, then made his way across Euston Road, coughing and wheezing whilst trying to negotiate the swarms of commuters, all desperate to get home. Arriving at Euston, he passed the bus station and considered taking the bus. It would make a pleasant change, but he would have to take two buses and spend almost twice as many hours travelling as he would on the Tube. No. He had better stick to his original plan.

Except the walk had made him thirsty; his last drink had been a cup of tea at around three o'clock. He sighed, he should really have brought a bottle of water for later, he would not be able to last the journey home feeling like this. He could really do with an ice-cold lager…and why not? There were plenty of pubs in the area, what better way to quench his thirst? Come to think of it, he could catch up with a few friends and colleagues from nearby University College while he was at it. The Tube could wait.

Soon he was joining the crowds of smokers and drinkers spilling out onto the pavements along Tottenham Court and the surrounding area. Then, a little later than planned, he was leaving his last pub, eventually arriving at Goodge Street Station at 9.20 p.m. Touching his blue Oyster travel card on the yellow reader, he made his way through the barriers to the lifts, which would take him down to the platforms. He was finally on his way home.

Even this late in the evening the station was busy, though not as crowded as on his usual journey. Two or three hours earlier, at least two trains would have passed by before he could access the platform edge, let alone get on a train. That said, despite there not being so many people around, it was still unbearably hot. The heat, endemic to these older, lower-level stations, had prompted portable, industrial-sized fans to be strategically placed around the platforms and public areas, to little effect. The London Mayor had even promised air conditioning, though everyone knew this would not be happening any time soon. Hopefully, there would not be too long a wait.

He looked up at the electronic display board. Good, the next train to Edgware via Charing Cross was only three minutes away. Two minutes passed. More people entered the platform. It was getting hotter. One minute to go. He counted down the seconds until, with a rush of hot air, the train came clattering into the station. Standing alongside the open door, with continuous 'mind the gap' announcements resonating in his ears, he waited for ten, perhaps fifteen, people to get off the train before he was jostled into a carriage by the incoming crowd. It was not until the train reached Belsize Park that he managed to find a seat, and after a long stressful day, coupled with several pints of lager, he was soon fast asleep.

A bright red sunset woke him, as the train moved above ground. During these lighter, summer nights, this was his favourite part of the journey, just looking out of the window and watching the world go by. As the train rattled past rows of houses, he thought of the people inside: settled down watching the evening's television, or a film perhaps; catching up with friends over a couple of beers and takeaway pizza, or heading to bed for an early night, in preparation for work the next morning.

They passed one house where all the upstairs windows were covered with black bin liners. Perhaps, he thought to himself, the inhabitants worked a nightshift and needed to block out the daylight...but surely it would make more sense to buy proper curtains? Then again, he had seen stranger things on his commutes home. Sometimes, if the houses were lower down, he could see into people's bedrooms. On those occasions he felt somewhat like a stalker, especially if the train was going slowly, which it occasionally did. The other night they had stopped just outside Golders Green, and as the train waited, he had witnessed a young couple being particularly intimate, through an attic room window. They were totally oblivious to the outside world, and what with the heatwave it had probably been too hot to close the windows and curtains. In any case, who would have thought someone might be watching from outside? Except he had been watching, and they had been too engrossed in one another to have noticed a stationary train just over the way. The other occupants of the house, the parents of one of the young lovers perhaps, had been sat downstairs in front of the television, oblivious to what was going on above their heads.

He must have drifted off to sleep again because the next thing he knew there was an automated female voice telling him they were approaching Colindale. Startled, he caught the arm of the girl sitting next to him, as he rushed to get up. Strange…he could have sworn she had not been there earlier. She had definitely not got on the train at the last station, he had only been dozing then, and would have noticed her sitting down next to him. Glancing down to apologise, he could not help but notice her penetrating stare. People travelling on the Underground usually tried to avoid eye contact, but this girl seemed determined to catch his attention. She was trying to say something, he was sure of that, though he could not work out for the life of him what it was. He had no time to ask. The doors had been open for some time now; he had only seconds to leave the train. Rapidly apologising, yet again, he made his way out of the door and onto the platform. Looking back, he noticed that the girl was still staring at him, and as the train pulled away her eyes did not leave his until the carriage was out of sight.

Who was she? Had he seen her before? He tried to think…she did look familiar, but why? Running through his daily commute, he concluded that she was not one of the regular travellers. Most people had a set routine, and even in a city as large as London, you tended to see the same faces almost every day. And she was not one of his students, or he would have recognised her instantly.

As he headed down the platform, he contemplated what had just happened. After years of travelling the same journey, day in day out, he knew the route out of the station like the back of his hand: a swift walk up the stairs, a few short steps, then a sharp left towards the exit. But tonight, something was different. He paced up the stairs as normal, but instead of there being a short walkway to the ticket barriers, his way is blocked by a solid wall. Stepping back in surprise, he was incensed by the sudden interruption. The wall had obviously been there for some time, years by the looks of it, and the once white paintwork was now a dull grey. Even the large 'Underground' roundel in the wall's centre had faded almost to invisibility. An unexpected development.

He weighed up the situation and resolved to try again. Hopefully, this time the wall would be gone, and he could be on his way. As he turned back towards the stairs, he thought of the girl. He had already expelled her from his mind, but she was back again, his academic curiosity fascinated by the mystery of her. He could do without this. He was tired, hungry, and just wanted to get home. Trying to expunge any thoughts of the girl, and empty his mind, he walked purposefully onward and promptly collided with someone coming from the opposite direction. He looked up. A white t-shirt. Blue, faded jeans. Yes, it was the same girl. Confused, he instinctively caught her arm before she could fall backwards down the stairs.

She took a few moments to regain her composure, but instead of acknowledging him, she simply reached out and gripped his wrist, smiling, before slowly walking away. Trying to speak was impossible: the shock of seeing her again and preventing her from falling down the stairs had left him dumbfounded. He had to forget about it. She clearly did not want to speak to him, and at that moment he was more interested in leaving the station…but his thoughts had other ideas, persistently returning to her as he continued back to the platform. Halfway down the staircase, he spun around, looking for her. She had disappeared. He peered down to the opposite platform, then along the walkway to the southbound trains. No, she was nowhere to be seen. It was only moments since they had met on the stairs…where had she gone?

As he made his way to the exit, the solid wall blocked his path again. This was frustrating. He had no desire to spend the night on the platform. Getting desperate, he repeated the process. Down to the platform, then back up the stairs. The same result. He tried again, and again, and again. He felt trapped.

After the fourth attempt, he was so exhausted from all the exertion that he decided to carry on to the next station, at Burnt Oak, and try there. No luck, nor at the terminus at Edgware: each time, the staircase led to nothing but an unyielding wall. Hendon, Brent Cross, Golders Green, Hampstead, Belsize Park…he tried all the stations southward, each time with the same result. By now, dismay was turning to anxiety. On arriving at Tottenham Court Road, he decided to change tack, catching a Central Line train to Holborn. But his exit was once again barred.

As with all deep level stations, instead of ticket barriers, the escalators led to a small, enclosed concourse, and he had no alternative but to return to the platform, any platform. But no matter how many platforms he visited, there was no exit. Giving up on the idea of taking a different line, he decided to catch the tube to Leicester Square, so he could pick up the Northern Line again and resume his normal journey home.

Reaching Colindale, he found his exit blocked again. The strange phenomenon continued as he retraced his route back to Tottenham Court Road, testing all the exits along the way. After so many hours of travelling, he was beginning to accept the hopelessness of the situation, and a bizarre calmness fell over him. Instead of rushing between stations, he started to take things slowly, travelling aimlessly above and below ground, from the main city to the less built-up suburban areas, losing all sense of time.

It seemed like forever ago since he had started travelling. He looked down at his watch. Still 9.40 p.m. The battery must have gone. His mobile phone was no help either, the screen was blank, strange given that it had been almost fully charged only a few hours ago. In an attempt to distract himself from this perplexing situation, he inspected the people around him: sleepy looking passengers clutching battered gift bags, clearly returning from visiting friends or relatives; partygoers just heading out for the evening; people curled up reading books, or staring at their phones; fast food workers, bar staff and night cleaners, all heading home after their long shifts, or on their way to start work for the evening. Many of the partygoers were drenched, it must have started raining outside. No sane person took a raincoat out to a nightclub.

Despite being surrounded by so many people, he felt lonely. He was a stranger, looking in on a world that was revolving around him, separate and distinct from his surroundings. The trains and platforms were at times busy, often overcrowded, but as soon as he reached the impassable wall that blocked his every exit, everyone around him seemed to vanish into thin air. At a loss and exhausted, he eventually fell asleep, the gentle rocking of the District Line train lulling him into unconsciousness.

Waking with a sudden start, he found himself in a much older carriage, which must have seen at least thirty to forty years of service. Dark, filthy, battered...the once clean fluorescent tubes were masked by a film of hardened dust, and the floor was a mass of dirt and discarded cigarette ends. Worse still, years of exposure to cigarette smoke had turned the white walls and ceiling to a horrible mustardy colour.

As he took in his new surroundings, he suddenly caught a glimpse of the girl in the white t-shirt again, sitting a few seats down on the opposite side of the carriage. She was reading, and on closer inspection he noticed that it was an academic book. As a seasoned scholar, he was impressed by how studiously she was scrutinising the book, constantly looking to the references at the back before either smiling or frowning as she considered what she had read. He was intrigued. This was the third time he had seen her, and he was beginning to ask himself whether she was real, or simply a figment of his imagination. After all, she had mysteriously reappeared when she came into his thoughts at the top of the stairs; then disappeared again when he went after her. He could not figure her out. What had she been trying to tell him earlier, when they had first met on the train at Colindale? Was she alright, after having almost been knocked down the stairs? He must speak to her.

As he rose from his seat, getting ready to go over to her, his attention was caught by a young boy dressed as a cowboy, shooting everyone around him with his toy gun. Too late, the train stopped, and she was one of the first to leave the carriage. Thoughts of approaching her evaporated as she made her way through the crowd on the platform. He could only admire her air of confidence, with her head held high and shoulders back.

The crowds of people had no option but to stand aside, as she moved along the platform with military precision.

Taking his seat again, he watched as she disappeared towards the exit. In all honesty, he probably would have looked foolish, a man of his age trying to approach an attractive young lady, especially without any pretext. He looked inside his case and pulled out a packet of cigarettes. He could not get used to the fact that people were smoking on the Underground. He was quite certain it had been banned years ago, after the King's Cross fire if he remembered correctly, but several people in his carriage had already lit up so he saw no reason why he shouldn't. There was one cigarette left. He had been planning on buying another pack when he left the station, which he might still be able to do when he eventually finished this incredible but depressing journey.

He relaxed into his seat, the cigarette smoke helping to clear his mind of the mystery girl, and continued his people watching. He had always been fascinated by people going about their daily lives, and began to note all the individuals in the carriage: the group of smart gentlemen in their pinstripe suits and bowler hats, engrossed in a variety of quality newspapers; the eccentric but not so sharply dressed man reading the *Evening News*, aided by a small magnifying glass; the courting couple, embracing one another, too absorbed to notice the elderly drunk who had just fallen off his seat onto the floor in the middle of the carriage; the small boy who stopped shooting his gun to watch the drunk man clumsily trying to lift himself back onto his seat; the boy's mother, mumbling in disgust, pushing her young son's gaze away from the scene.

He stopped, suddenly realising why this carriage felt so odd. There was always a shortage of trains, and old carriages were often pressed back into service. But people smoking? The clothes they were wearing? The *Evening News* the man was reading? That newspaper had been out of circulation for years. This could not be the modern day. He picked up a discarded newspaper, studying the front page. The date was wrong. Today was a Wednesday, but the newspaper insisted it was Thursday. And none of the stories looked familiar. He squinted to look at the actual date. It was still May the ninth, but the year…the year was 1957.

After a solid ten minutes of panic, he calmed himself. He was trapped on a train, sixty years in the past. It was surreal, yes, but he would have to accept the situation, or else he would surely go mad. He knew for certain that his exit would be blocked by a solid wall again, so he might as well take in his surroundings. After four or five hours of travelling, he began to realise that life on the Underground in 1957 was not that much different to what he was used to. On one platform, two police constables were attempting to arrest a youth who was clearly the worse for drink. He could easily have seen the same scene a few days ago on his way home; only the policemen's uniforms would have been different.

The people on the Tube seemed to be behaving much the same, keeping themselves to themselves, rarely interacting with other passengers. When there was interaction, he strained his ears, trying to listen in on the conversation. In one carriage, he witnessed a couple arguing over some love tryst the man had been having with the woman's friend, while in another a group of tourists were discussing which attraction to visit first: the National Gallery, Westminster Abbey or St Paul's Cathedral.

Another hour went by as the carriages began to fill up, and he was eventually forced to surrender his seat to an elderly lady. He was used to having to stand; back in his own time, most peak-time journeys on the detestable Northern Line necessitated standing. He was regularly pressed against passengers who refused to use a handkerchief, coughing and sneezing all over him, or sweat-drenched commuters, especially during the hot weather.

Even now, in 1957, the carriage was growing increasingly hot and stuffy as more people tried to cram themselves in. No change there then, other than the consolation of not having to suffer the infernal racket of tinny music, coming from several headphones at once. Mobile phones and personal stereos had not been invented, nor had the large rucksacks which modern students and tourists seemed to insist on using. Another consolation, not having a giant rucksack being shoved in your face as people tried to move around the carriage.

Waking after yet another deep sleep, he found himself in an even older carriage, which looked just like one he had seen in a transport museum. The brutal harshness of fluorescent tube lights had given way to the warm glow of candescent light bulbs, and instead of plastic and metal the carriage was composed of polished wood. Even the seats were a more temperate orange-red colour, compared to the cold blue seat covers that he was used to.

The man opposite was reading a copy of *The Times,* and he could just make out the date: the ninth of May 1907. He watched closely as the train stopped outside each station. The people were now more formally dressed; gone was the eclectic mix of formal suits, jeans, and t-shirts. Instead, the outfits were smart and more regimented: suits, overcoats, ankle-length dresses, hats…he realised how strange he must look in his modern, semi-casual attire.

After dismissing his self-consciousness, he began to adjust to his new circumstances, and continued to travel the length and breadth of the network. Some stations he was acquainted with, others he was not. Some had just been built and would later be abandoned as the network developed. He thought of the book he was about to publish; though it was too late to make any major changes, this little adventure would have proved useful during his research. This was one of the most important periods in the Underground's history. While the main network was mostly in place in the early 1900s, there was still a significant portion yet to be added. This was the period before Frank Pick, the man who founded the modern London Transport system and who was credited for bringing different train companies together, and before Holden who provided the art deco designs for Pick's new stations.

He tried to imagine what the city outside looked like. The street layout would be the same, but the Second World War had not yet happened, and neither had the First come to think of it, so the post-war reconstruction which radically changed the face London would not have happened yet. He was fascinated to see Britain at the turn of the twentieth century, and to witness the last vestiges of the steam-powered nineteenth century. With the internal combustion engine still in its infancy, everything above ground would be mostly horse-drawn, with a few early motorised vehicles. Some of the main roads might now be electrically lit, but many of the side streets would still have gas lighting. With the modern electric train now in its ascendency, the trains he was travelling on would be considered ultra-modern by his fellow passengers.

An argument between a young couple rudely interrupted him from yet another sleep. He was angry about the abrupt awakening, but the early morning sunlight pouring into the bright, airy carriage soon lifted his spirits. On this occasion, his deep sleep had not resulted in any dramatic changes to his surroundings and had left him feeling refreshed and optimistic. He was determined to figure out what was happening to him.

In this strange reality, he only seemed to grow despondent when he was tired, and after some sleep he always felt stronger and more capable of thinking things through. He noted that his situation appeared to change almost every time he awoke; not only was he travelling back in time, but on most occasions the time of day also changed. When he fell asleep at night, he woke in the daylight; when he nodded off during the day, he would wake in the dark. Based on this, he could not help but conclude that the service must be running constantly, which was peculiar. He would have expected the service to stop by midnight, and for a member of staff to appear and turn him off the train, or for the train to return to the depot where the night staff would have done much the same. At this point, he would have welcomed being thrown off the network, anything to escape this endless travelling.

Despite the service never appearing to cease, whenever he woke in the morning the carriages had all been washed and swept, ready for another day of service. He could not understand how they could clean the carriages so thoroughly without him noticing. Not only that, but time seemed strangely altered, with what must have been hours spent travelling compressed into just minutes. Overall, there was no rhyme or reason to what was happening. He sighed, sinking deeper into his seat, the feelings of despair he had hoped to banish washing over him in a great wave of hopelessness.

He had never been one to dream, his sleep usually went uninterrupted. But perhaps his exhaustion had prompted him to dream up this nightmare…perhaps this would all end as soon as he reached Colindale, and he would wake up just in time to get off the train? Whether this was a dream or not, everything certainly seemed real.

He suddenly remembered reading a paper by one Dr Susan Salem. Well, it had been something like that anyway, he had always struggled with names. She had argued that, while dreaming, the subconscious often created a state of existence so real it was difficult, if not impossible, to differentiate it from reality. These ideas were well beyond him, he was a historian after all, not a psychologist. But he was somewhat fascinated by her proposal; it would be interesting to meet her and discuss her paper in more detail, especially after this experience, if it did turn out to be a dream. Conversations with other academics always interested him, and who knows, they might have something in common. He did recall someone once telling him that she also had an interest in history; he was sure he could interest her in some of his areas of research, whilst possibly acting as a case study for her research into dreams.

For the next hour, he amused himself with thoughts of Dr Salem. First, he imagined her as a frumpy school swot, with greasy hair and thick rimmed spectacles, going through several other possibilities before settling on a confident, athletic, nubile young lady, who all the boys at school and university had wanted to date. This last incarnation brought a smile to his face, making him want to meet her even more. Indeed, imagining them being together proved a pleasant distraction from his erstwhile predicament. It was only when his imagination grew cruder, and their meetings began to go well beyond what was professionally prudent, that he shifted his thoughts elsewhere. After all, she was most likely a lot younger than him.

Refocusing his mind on the present journey, he noted the mixture of familiar and unfamiliar stations they passed along the way: Hounslow Barracks to Uxbridge, Barking on the Metropolitan District Line, and Verney Junction to Elephant and Castle on the Metropolitan and Bakerloo lines. He was now on the Bakerloo Line, and remembered journeying on this line to visit Wembley, to watch the FA Cup Final. He could not do that now, in 1907. The line was yet to be extended that far, and the stadium had not been built.

He hopped off the train at Edgware Road, deciding to head back towards Oxford Circus, where he could pick up the Northern Line. On the platform, a flash of white caught his eye. Could it be? Yes, it was her, the girl in the white t-shirt again. She was hurrying towards the exit, but it would have been a waste of time going after her. There were too many people on the platform, and she was too far ahead, he would never catch up. He had missed her again.

His reasonable mood from a few moments ago vanished, and he was once again consumed by misery and confusion. He had resigned himself to being trapped on the Underground; accepted the time travelling as some form of strange reality...but his persistent sightings of this mystery girl? He could not comprehend anything with certainty now. Taking a deep breath, he resolved to forget her, pressing on with his bleak, endless journey.

At the interchange between lines, he stopped to study a wall-mounted map of the Underground network. Not the simplified Beck map of later years, but a much cruder version, comprising a mass of similar coloured lines which wove their way around the Capital like spaghetti. After a while, he managed to find the Hampstead Tube, which nowadays was known as the Northern Line. Without his historical knowledge of the London Tube system he would most certainly have lost himself a while ago, for almost all the station names differed from their modern counterparts. What he knew as Tottenham Court Road in 2007 was named Oxford Street on this 1907 map, and Goodge Street station was labelled as Tottenham Court Road. It was all very confusing. Worse still, he could only travel as far as Golders Green, since his usual route had not been built yet.

It was the guard's cry of 'Paddington station! Paddington station! All change please!' that woke him. Apparently, they had reached the terminus...but finishing at Paddington? He could have sworn they had much further to go. He felt groggy after another deep sleep but managed to drag himself into consciousness and look around him. A brightly polished carriage made of wood. He had to think fast, the guard would throw him off at any moment now...the first Underground line had opened in around 1860, 1863 to be exact, and he remembered reading that it too had terminated at Paddington...and given that this carriage was in pristine condition...yes, that would make sense. He must have travelled back to sometime in the late nineteenth century.

As he stepped onto the platform, he gasped in awe. Nothing recreated in a museum could compete with the vibrant brilliance of a newly created original masterpiece. This station, which many historians considered to be the birthplace of the London Underground, was akin to a cathedral, and would remain almost unchanged well into the twentieth century.

Unfortunately, the station's grandeur was somewhat diminished by the lack of light. Despite the vast, arched glass roof and enormous side-mounted windows, deliberately designed to let in as much daylight as possible, it was currently night-time and the station was relying on gas for illumination. This might have been adequate for the locals, but he was used to electric lighting and was struggling with the dimness. It would take some getting used to, especially since everything would soon become blackened with the soot produced by locomotives.

Unsurprisingly, his exit from the station was barred, and the signs directing him to another way out only led him back onto the platform. There was no option but to hop on the next train, which was just pulling into the station. No one appeared to take much notice of the steam choking the station, though the novelty of the new service was made evident by how long everyone took to herd themselves into the open carriages. From his research, he already knew about the different classes of travel that had once been prevalent on the Underground, and now he was here, experiencing this long-gone, deferential, class-ridden society for himself.

He joined a small number of passengers climbing into one of the enclosed first-class carriages at the rear, found himself a seat, and settled down for the journey. After all the distress and confusion of his previous journeys, this one felt different; he was finding the experience rather fascinating. He thought of his research; how much this strange situation had informed his understanding of this time period; what the journey ahead might bring…it was exciting!

Glancing at the wealthy nineteenth-century Londoner's, the men in their formal frock coats and top hats, and the women in their long heavy dresses, he considered how out of place he must look among them. At least he was dressed for the weather, unlike his fellow passengers, who were entirely unsuitably dressed for a hot summer's day such as this one.

He suddenly thought of the mystery girl, and how out of place she too would look in this nineteenth century carriage. Within moments, the girl herself came into view, as if his thought had summoned her. She was sitting further along the carriage, wearing a black leather jacket over her t-shirt, looking just as out of place as he did. Seeing her again instantly lifted his spirits, and he was determined to seize this opportunity to approach her and talk to her. After all, she must be experiencing this exciting new experience too; she might know what was going on, and how to get back to the modern world. The train was about to depart, so there was little chance of her escaping again. Dismissing his nerves, he was preparing himself to walk towards her when her gaze suddenly met his. As soon as she saw him, she dropped back into her seat, hiding behind the rotund woman beside her. It was clear that she did not want to be noticed. His thoughts of approaching her disappeared as quickly as they had arrived. It was probably best to leave her alone; causing a scene would only draw attention, and that was the last thing he wanted to do.

The guard blew his whistle and off they went. With the windows now just narrow slits, the guard's announcements were his only means of determining where the train was; it felt not unlike twenty-first century London, only with a human guide rather than automated electronic announcements. And it was much better than his 1957 experience, when his only guidance had been the maps above the carriage windows.

He decided to travel to the line's other terminus, at Farringdon Street, before returning through King's Cross, Gower Street, Portland Road, Baker Street and

Edgware to Paddington. What else could he do? There was little opportunity to explore the Underground system, this one solitarily line was all that existed at this time. Besides, it was growing late, the service would be finishing soon. He needed to figure out what to do next…might he fall asleep and awake the next day again?

His lack of ticket was beginning to concern him. During the quiet periods, the guards seemed reluctant to inspect tickets, but what if his luck did not last? Given his inability to reach street level, he had no means of purchasing a ticket. Even his Oyster travel card would be of no use; how would he explain to the conductor that this small piece of plastic entitled him to unlimited travel? Plastic had not even been invented yet! The money in his pocket would also be of little use in this pre-decimal age; it would most likely be treated as a foreign currency. Would the conductor call for assistance, the police, perhaps? Or would he simply be thrown off the train, out of the station even? That last thought sounded inviting. At least he would finally be rid of this perpetual entrapment…except that he would then be trapped nearly one hundred and fifty years in the past, with nowhere to live, no money, no friends, no relatives…the thought was terrifying. But at least he would be free, to a certain extent. Jumping off the train, he decided to try and leave the station, once more for luck and all that.

On reaching the top of a long stairway, he once again followed the exit signs, half expecting his way to be blocked. Which it was, but on this occasion, as he turned to retrace his steps back to the platform, he found the stairs had been replaced by a small doorway. He could do nothing but enter. Once through, he found himself in a large empty room, the black and white tiled floor, and oak panelled walls peppered by ornate oil lamps, in keeping with the period. After several cautious steps he looked back, but instead of the doorway and station, all he could see was an opening, beyond which was nothing but blackness. His primal instinct was firmly against the option of turning back into what was now a black abyss, so he had no choice but to continue through the room.

On the other side of the tiled space was another door, though this time it was closed. He turned the antiquated brass handle and the door swung open, to reveal a more modern-looking, electrically lit room, with a two-tone Art-Deco paint scheme. The walls and ceiling were discoloured by years of neglect, and it was clear that this room had not been as well kept as the first. On one side of the room were a triage of windows, looking out onto what appeared to be another railway station.

He walked up to the nearest window; the sun was shining, and based on the scene before him, it was sometime during the early twentieth century. By now he had become used to trying to assess peculiar situations, and as usual he had no answers, only more questions. He began to wave his arms frantically, banging on the window, but no one on the platform took any notice of him. Could they even see him? Could they see the window? Did it exist for them? The last thought lingered with him, and he concluded that the window almost certainly did not exist for the people outside. After all, they appeared totally unaware of its existence; to them it was probably just another wall.

Looking closer, he noticed that some of the people were wearing clothes from different time periods. Were they trapped like him? He felt a wave of relief, he might not be alone! Others too might be experiencing this lonely and ensnared existence. But even if this was the case, what next? He could not go back any further in time, for he had already reached the earliest point in the history of the Underground. Perhaps these rooms were taking him to the next stage, whatever that might be? With a sudden flash of optimism, he decided to test his hypothesis, despite the whole idea being purely conjecture, to see whether stepping from one room to the next would eventually lead him back to his own time.

As he continued to wander through a series of similar rooms, he noticed that each one looked out onto stations, mirroring the names of those he had passed through on his most recent train journey. Eventually, the endless rooms and doorways ended, and he made his way through the stone arches of a medieval walkway, carrying on walking until he arrived at an equally old, huge, domed hall. Its enormity was difficult to comprehend, with columns stretching far into the darkness of the ceiling. Yet, as his eyes gradually adjusted to the gloom, he could make out the outlines of other people in the hall, standing as individuals, in pairs or in small groups. Disturbingly, he could see from their mannerisms that they were all oblivious to everyone around them.

As he began to move amongst them, he was deafened by a mass of incoherent whisperings. Those in pairs or groups were displaying some sort of reverence to the place, and seemed frightened of raising their voices, whilst the individuals seemed afraid of talking to anyone else. Or perhaps they were indifferent to the situation. Either way, he sensed that everyone was in their own private bubble, where no one existed other than themselves or their small group.

How long they had been there was impossible to tell, though on closer inspection he could see that they were all from different time periods. They were similar to the people he had seen at the stations, through the invisible windows, except these people were from a much wider span of time periods: medieval, early modern, eighteenth century, nineteenth century…Some were dressed in modern clothing, and others in styles and fabrics he had never seen before, perhaps from the future?

At first, the people appeared to be moving haphazardly, but after a while, he noticed they were all channelling themselves in specific directions of travel. All of them seemed to be moving towards small banks of lights, around the hall's circumference. He felt the pull too, and what at first were small pin heads in the distance gradually became other doorways. Above each doorway, through which the groups of people were being funnelled, was a date and time. Once again, he wondered how long they had been kept waiting before being summoned to their allotted doorway. Perhaps, like him, they had only recently arrived…or perhaps they had been here for centuries. As he drew closer, he quickly spotted his doorway. Date: the ninth of May. Time: 9.40 p.m.

Drifting through, he realised that the hall was just a holding area, as he discovered another dark hall on the other side of his doorway. Well, it was more of a room this time: narrower, lower, with the only light coming from the large viewing screens which ran along each of the walls. Taking his time to look at the first couple of screens, he concluded that each was a three-dimensional image, showing a specific aspect of his life. The room had a smattering of alcoves decorated with similar screens, not just on the walls, but also on the floors.

He stopped at the first alcove. The screens were showing his childhood. Carefully touching one to see what they were made of his hand passed through some sort of membrane, and as his hand broke the barrier, it activated the sound of the memory. He toyed with the idea of jumping through, to join the scene on display. But the screens might only be one way to escape, and he might become trapped in that moment of his past, with no chance of returning. Worse still, he would immediately meet his younger self. Based on all the science fiction films he had seen, meeting another version of oneself always ended badly, and could lead to some terrible paradoxes.

Taking his hand out of the screen, he went to inspect the rest of the room. His entire existence was there: nursery; primary school; senior school; sixth-form; university; the whole of his academic career; close friends; colleagues; acquaintances; scenes, some explicit, of him with former girlfriends, during his misspent youth when he spread his seed with carefree abandon...his ex-wife, Susan, standing with his daughter and granddaughter. He stopped, staring at that one scene. He did not recognise the moment, though from the authenticity of the previous images he had to assume it was a true representation. It upset him, seeing Jane, and his granddaughter, Florence. It had been a long time since they had been together, and he felt guilty for never keeping in proper contact after the divorce. Perhaps this was a reminder, prompting him to make amends? He made a mental note to get in touch with his daughter once he had escaped this nightmare journey.

He carried on walking. All the recesses and sections of the room were dedicated to a specific theme, and he came across one that consisted of all the exhibitions he had ever visited. He was tempted to spend hours in this section, but resisted, knowing he must press on. Next was a set of screens highlighting aspects to his research: the archives and libraries he had visited; a montage of the documents he had used; the people he had interviewed. On the final screen was the seminar he had presented earlier that day. Once again, he considered passing through the screen. After all, it was so close to the present time…perhaps he could stand at the back and sneak out? It was a plan. But was it worth the risk? No. Probably not.

He passed by a couple more screens until he came across one showing the entrance to Goodge Street Tube Station, where he had started this bizarre journey. He peered at the screen, watching the people coming and going through the ticket barriers. Nothing seemed out of the ordinary. Then, out of nowhere, the figure of a man appeared on the far left of the concourse. There was no visible doorway, so whoever he was, he had apparently appeared out of thin air. He could not have walked through the main entrance, otherwise he would have been seen passing through the barriers. Nor could he have arrived from the platforms, for again, he would have been noticed.

He watched as the man made his way forward and stopped, just in front of him, appearing dazed and confused. The man's outfit was not dissimilar to his own: cream summer jacket, checked shirt, and an identical brown leather case. He continued watching as the man bent forward, as if to pick something up off the floor. But there was nothing there. He was trying to determine the reason for this strange behaviour when the man looked up, and he was finally able to get a clear view of the stranger's face. He stepped backwards in shock. It was his own face. He was the man in the screen.

He wanted to shout out, to catch his own attention, but before he could muster the courage to do so, the man who was himself looked at his watch, shrugged his shoulders and moved towards the platforms. Watching himself walk away, he stood for a moment, collecting his thoughts. He had no recollection of the moment he had just witnessed, but the outfit had been identical to the one he was wearing now. Was this a prediction, perhaps? Was his journey about to end? Would he finally be able to go home? The thought excited him, and with his spirits lifted, he decided to move on.

There were no more screens, so he carried on walking, feeling hopeful. After a few minutes he came to a modern, brightly lit passage, with a moving walkway. In the distance was a brilliant white light. He approached slowly, letting the walkway carry him. His next thought frightened him: could this bright light be the end; the entrance to the afterlife? He wanted to turn back, but he was now too far along the walkway. It would take forever to walk against the flow, and in any case, he could no longer see where he had come from, not even a speck in the distance. Trepidation began to build up as he drew closer, quickly subsiding as he realised that the light was coming from an automatic door.

As the door opened, he found himself on another station concourse. A small, recognisable concourse. He was back at Goodge Street Station. This must have been the scene he witnessed on that last screen. There was a feeling of déjà vu as he bent down to lift a free *London Lite* evening paper from one of the receptacles next to the ticket barriers. Looking at the date, he saw that it was still May the ninth.

He folded the paper to read later, looking down at his watch. It was working again, and the time read 9.21 p.m., roughly the time he had first arrived at the station. Engulfed by surprise and shock, he considered going outside for another stiff drink. But no, he would sooner get home, and with a swift pace he began to make his way to the platforms.

He felt uneasy about alighting at Colindale, and as he climbed to the top of the stairway from the platform, he gingerly peered to the left. But this time, there was no brick wall, just the short walk to the ticket barriers. He touched his Oyster card on the reader and felt a sensation of euphoria as the barriers opened before him.

In the small station grocery shop, Mohamed asked if he had been working late, as he handed over a packet of cigarettes with a smile. Too tired to explain what had happened, and not sure he would be believed, he simply returned the smile and promised to see Mohamed the next day.

Outside in the setting sun, he turned right onto Colindale Avenue, passing the hairdressers and the grocery shop, the local greasy spoon, and the newspaper library. He was almost home. At 9.55 p.m., about the time he should have been home in the first place, he put his key in the door.

He could not remember the last time he had eaten a meal. He could really do with some food, but all he really wanted to do was get into bed and fall deeply asleep. Making his way to his bedroom, he lay on his bed, falling swiftly into semi-consciousness. But he could not stop his mind from going over his experience. Perhaps it *had* all been a dream, days and hours compressed into those short minutes between Golder's Green and Colindale? Contemplating the whole incredible journey, his mind eventually settled on the room of screens. In the safety of his bed, he began to reflect on the messages they could have been telling him.

His existence had been laid out before him, as if his entire life had been recorded and played back. Reminding him of his successes, failures, hopes, ambitions, loves, losses, personal and professional achievements. There had been other messages too: mistakes he had made in his youth; errors in his later life, especially the lack of contact with his family. There was too much to comprehend at this late hour. But as much as he tried to expunge the thoughts from his mind, he could not escape them, especially the memory of that penultimate screen: his seminar presentation. It lingered over and over, becoming a nightmare as he tried to fall sleep. Then, suddenly, in the front row of the audience, there she was: the girl with the white t-shirt. The same girl he had kept seeing, on the train, on the stairs at Colindale, in 1957, 1907 and again in 1863.

She was taking over his mind. She intrigued him. The mystery of her illusiveness, how he would have liked to talk to her, to know her better. Regrets of not approaching her when he had the chance. She was still troubling him as he finally drifted off to sleep.

A few hours later he suddenly returned to consciousness, sensing a presence in the room. Half asleep, he opened his eyes to see the girl standing in front of the closed bedroom door. He was shocked. How was she here, in his room? Usually, there was a loud creak when the door opened, which would have been enough to wake him, but this time there had been no sound.

After a moment, the shock subsided, and their eyes met. He had no idea what she was thinking, but he knew for sure what was on his mind. She was beautiful. A noise came from outside the door, probably the cat knocking something over on the landing. Startled, the girl turned, and as she did so, he saw a trace of what looked like a tattoo running down her back. The hallway was silent again, her panic slowly diminishing. She turned back to face him, taking a step forward. Now illuminated by the streetlight outside, he had a better view of her, and as he studied her more closely, he was struck not just by the slenderness of her figure, but by the youthfulness of her boyish appearance.

He stared at her, silently in awe of her tanned, possibly Mediterranean complexion. She seemed too perfect to be true. Most likely in her early twenties, and with cropped dark hair, she was shorter than he remembered. In an instant, he was lusting after her androgyne. He imagined them making love together, time after time until exhaustion. Since his divorce there had been the odd one-night stand but nothing more, and right now he would give anything for her to climb into his bed and lay beside him.

Sitting up, his mind was a compendium of questions. Who was she? Why had she latched onto him? How did she travel through time? How had she managed to get inside his house, his room? She took a few more steps towards him, until she was standing next to the bed. He went to speak, only to be stopped by her finger on his lips. The finger caressed his face and she bent forward, brushing her lips against his. The thought of her beauty allowed him to surrender, as her lips lightly wrapped around his. He could sense the softness of her tongue as it tentatively searched for his own, and soon their mouths and tongues were fighting for supremacy. She took his hand, compelling him to explore her t-shirted body. He started with her chest, where the feel of a hardened nipple informed him that she was not wearing a brassier. Expectant of her near nakedness, he began to investigate further.

Climbing out of bed and pulling her towards him, he could feel the warm smoothness of her skin as he slid his hand under her shirt, which she quickly removed to reveal a slight, muscular body. Not overly muscular so as to make her unattractive, but just enough to ignite his excitement. Aroused, he reached out to rub the back of his hand against her flat stomach. Touching; feeling; his eyes travelling down to her jeans where he started to imagine the treasures he might find if he were to explore further.

He returned his gaze to her upper body, absorbing every detail like a child with a new toy. He had only just been fantasizing about her, and now here she was, almost naked in his arms. He twisted her round and stared at her from behind. She giggled shyly, his finger tracing the tattoo of a snake which twisted the full length of her back: from just below the beltline of her jeans, along her spine to the base of her neck, before slithering back down to her hip, then twisting back up her side, to rest its head on a firm, compact breast, lashing its bright red tongue against an almost black nipple. Why she should be so shy at this late stage was unfathomable. Was there a story behind the tattoo? Was she conscious of her small breasts, perhaps?

His thoughts dissipated as she moved closer, and they shared a deep kiss. One of his hands stroked her neck while the other slid under her jeans, to caress the firmness of her behind. Unfastening the top buttons of her jeans, she took his hand from her neck and guided it to the opening she had just created. Releasing her lips from his, she watched him touch and explore the delicate texture of her briefs, expelling a small gasp as he slid his fingers beneath the fabric to find the treasure he had been thinking of.

She pressed her hand against his, holding it in place, allowing him to take possession of his loot. He could sense her excitement as she pushed him onto the bed, where they spent an eternity playing; exploring one another. Three times they made love. Twice where she was in command, controlling, using him to quench an insatiable appetite. Three, four hours and they were done: him having spent his seed in a finale of frenzied sex, her having exhausted her stamina.

They remained in each other's arms, resting, regrouping, before she straddled him, ready for a fourth round.

He woke with a start. He was back on a Tube train as it pulled into Colindale station. The girl with the white t-shirt was sitting opposite, reading a book. She looked up and gave a half smile, before returning to her book. He smiled back. Searching for something to say seemed like a waste of time, the doors were open, and he had only seconds to leave the carriage. He was still staring at the girl as he stepped onto the platform. She lifted her head, and this time returned a full smile. It was too late: the doors had closed, and the train was about to leave.

He walked up the stairs towards the exit, and on reaching the top he looked over the opposite stairway to watch the train as it left the station towards Burnt Oak and Edgware. His mind was still with the girl as he turned towards the exit. He was immediately confronted with a solid wall. He stood, frozen, staring at the obstruction with incredulity, and turned to look at the platform, contemplating what to do next…

*

At approximately 9.55 p.m., on the evening of Wednesday the ninth of May, 2007, the body of fifty-six-year-old Professor Mitchell Povey was found slumped in the seat of a Northern Line train, as it arrived at the terminus in Edgware. The duty pathologist estimated the time of death as sometime between nine-thirty p.m. and 9.55 p.m. A later post-mortem revealed that Povey had died of a massive heart attack, undoubtedly bought on by years of drinking and heavy smoking. Death would have been almost instantaneous, stated the pathologist at the inquest. There would have been no pain, simply the sensation of falling asleep.

His partial replacement at the University of London was twenty-six-year-old Dr Sara Salem. Specialising in psychology, she was already an accomplished researcher with numerous papers on the workings of the subconscious during dreams having already been published. All had received rave reviews in the academic press; so too had her doctoral thesis, which argued that immediately after death the mind continued in a dreamlike state, creating a subconscious reality which the patient would be unable to distinguish from real life.

Talented as she was, her new colleagues were somewhat apprehensive about a young person being appointed to such an important position. Rushed into taking on some of Povey's history teaching, the Professor's former students were also surprised at the youth of his replacement. At the start of the new autumn term, they had assumed she was a new student joining the class, and it was not until she had removed her black three-quarter length leather jacket, taking her place behind the lectern, that they realised she was to be their new lecturer. Even then, they were fascinated, especially the male students, by her torn Levi jeans and flimsy white t-shirt — under which could be seen the outline of a twisting snake.

Sis

Straight off the street and through the front door. Yes. It was the same house. It was old, every house in the street was old, but this house was the best. The others had walls darkened by damp; mildew on the windows; rain coming in through the roof...but not this house. It needed decorating, of course: the wallpaper was from a past age, and the paint was peeling in places. But beyond that, the house was clean and tidy, which was all that mattered. Mother made sure of that.

It was a dark dreary day and Mother was in the yard, putting the washing through the mangle ready for the line, hoping to get it done before the rain came. Father was in the front room, sleeping under the paper. It must be Saturday afternoon; the pub had probably just closed, and he was sleeping off the lunchtime session.

With no work to go to, he went twice on a Saturday: when the pub opened at eleven a.m. and then again at seven p.m.; he usually stayed until throwing out time. No sign of Sis. Of course not. It was a Saturday; she would be at work. The date was unclear, but she had started her Saturday job at Woolworths when she turned fifteen, so it must sometime be after that. Mother had been pleased; it would help with the house keeping. Father, too. More beer money for him, he had said.

Summer. The sun was shining, and Mother was again hanging out the washing, sheets this time. She had a smile on her face, despite struggling against a strong summer breeze. She should really have asked Father to help, but 'let him sleep' had been her regular excuse, 'then we can all get some peace and quiet.' That was probably why she looked so happy. Father was asleep; when he was asleep, he was harmless.

Mother was in the kitchen, looking serene as she carefully laid out everything ready for tea. Stew, as usual, though occasionally they had kippers if they were cheap enough at Uncle Ken's shop. Still no Sis. Ah, there she was, just coming through the front door. A few words of greeting then she went upstairs, probably to change out of her work uniform. She came down and

Mother was waiting at the table. Just Sis and Mother, Father was probably in the pub. The scene looked tranquil as they start eating. Peaceful. But the atmosphere was strained. They were not talking, not serious talk anyway, just trivial things: school, the weather, her job at Woolworths...as though there was an elephant in the room, and they were both trying their hardest to avoid it.

Winter. Snow on the ground. Mother was in the kitchen, bruises on her face, a black eye. Father must have had another one of his tempers. Sis was again coming in through the door. She asked what happened. Mother started crying. Sis cried too. It was not the first time this had happened. Usually there were no tears, it must have been serious this time.

The house was in darkness. It looked like Christmas time. Multi-coloured paper chains decorated the walls and ceiling; an unlit tree was standing in the corner of the living room; cards from friends and family sat on the mantelpiece. Just as the clock struck twelve, the front door opened and Father stumbled in from the pub, fumbling in the darkness. There was dark shadow behind him, not his, that of another man. Father shushed the shadow as they struggled up the narrow staircase. It was difficult to see who the other man was in the dark. He was entering Sis's room.

The dark shadow was leaving Sis's room, walking silently down the staircase and out the front door. Followed, tried to catch up to see who it was, but could not keep up. Down Frederick Street, Henrietta Street, Forest Gardens, then the High Street, where the dark shadow disappeared into an alleyway between two dowdy shops.

Sis's room. Sis sobbing on the bed, nightclothes raised to reveal parts of her anatomy no one was supposed to see. There was an eternity of silent weeping. Eventually, she fell asleep amongst the defiled mess around her.

Sunshine and summer dresses, joyful looks, betrayed by the atmosphere as Mother and Sis walked silently along the street to the pub on the corner. Sis stood waiting outside as Mother walked through the door. The pained look of anticipation on Sis's face was excruciating to observe, something bad was going to happen.

Mother and Father, arguing outside the pub. A crowd had gathered to watch the spectacle. Mother's blows started falling. Father was defenceless to retaliate, too many people about for him to be seen striking a woman. Mother stopped, turning to the crowd. She screamed something while pointing to Sis's swollen tummy. Father shook his head, holding up his hands in denial as the crowd's stare alternated between him and Sis's bump. Mother was still screaming as she dragged Sis away. Father's head was shaking as he retreated into the pub. A couple of men started to follow, to be held back by their women. Better not to get involved, they had said.

Mother and Sis were in the kitchen, Sis sitting by the table, clutching her now huge stomach. Mother was screaming for Father, who came running into the kitchen. 'Fetch Aunty Jenifer' was Mother's command, as she tried to console Sis, now crying out in agony.

First running, then sprinting, Father left Frederick Street, Henrietta Street then Forest Gardens, finally arriving at the High Street where he entered an old grocer's shop. He forced his way past a group of bemused housewives, angry at being pushed aside, so he could be at the head of the queue. Fighting for breath, he addressed the woman behind the counter. Aunty Jenifer. Turning quickly, she shouted to Uncle Ken at the counter opposite. Uncle Ken's face was white as he called Father to one side for a whispered conference. Aunty Jenifer collected a bag from the kitchen and rushed out of the shop.

Sis was on a make-shift bed in the front room. Aunty Jenifer had just arrived. Blankets, towels, hot water, more towels, and then a baby, a boy. Father and Uncle Ken had arrived just in time for the birth. Mother ordered them both out of the house.

Night-time, Father was coming through the front door, drunk as usual, except this time with scars and bruises. Mother was waiting, screaming as he entered the room, ordering him upstairs to see Sis.

Summer sunshine. A child looking well, at least two years old, a bundle of energy playing in the sun, while Mother hung out the washing. Sis was nowhere to be seen. Throughout the pregnancy, Woolworth's had kept her job open, so she was most likely there. Father was in the front room, snoozing under the paper, undoubtedly sleeping off another lunchtime session.

The school playground: children playing happily, except for a group of teasing troublemakers. Usually, it was his dinner money they were after, or they were badgering him to do their homework. Today was different. Derogatory remarks regarding his family.

'How's ya mam?' came the first shout.

'How's ya sis?'

Then the repeated chant, 'We know who your mam is, we know who your mam is, we know who your mam is ...' Several times, until— 'We know who your dad is, we know who your dad is, we know who your dad is...'

On and on and on until one miscreant finally hollered, 'When's ya sis gonna fetch you a brother from the grocers then?'

Troubled Mind

It had been a difficult day. First, the meeting with the Prime Minister had not gone at all well. Though the PM had offered his help, demanding a resignation was not entirely out of the question. Then, despite his Constituency Chairman and Parliamentary Advisor also promising their support, neither they, nor his solicitor, had much hope of him coming through unscathed. The truth was he had been mixing with the wrong people; associating with some rather disreputable characters, and tomorrow he would have to answer for it.

In bed at his Westminster flat, he had already set his radio alarm to come on at six a.m., so now it was just a case of getting off to sleep…easier said than done. It was probably the nightcap of several brandies with his Parliamentary Adviser which had tipped him over the edge; he should have known that sleep was usually impossible after having so much to drink. No matter how many times he willed himself into unconsciousness he just could not drift off. His mind was in a frustratingly dark place. Waves of negativity were rushing through his brain as he worried over what the next day would bring. Fears for his future political career; press coverage; how the fallout would affect his family. His mind was in freefall. Soon, sinister thoughts took over. Thoughts of taking the easy way out: more alcohol, perhaps, with pills; jumping out of the window…after all, he was on the eighteenth floor.

Time passed and the effects of the alcohol began to wear off, easing his mind a little. A tranquiliser would help. Except his doctor had been emphatic that they were not to be taken with or after alcohol. He sighed, trying to clear his mind. He had to take control, it was the only way he would get to sleep. Deep breaths. Think of nothing. Nothing but nothing. It was helping, his mind was growing clearer. The dark thoughts were still there, yes, but not as bad. Eventually, he fell into an uneasy sleep, first blankness, emptiness. Then the dreams began.

It was twilight amid a barren landscape. Pushing, pushing hard, pushing harder, and still the boulder refused to move. He had been trying for some time, not sure how much time. Trying for no reason, just to get the hard piece of rock moving. He stood up, looked about. The greyness was depressing, barely any visible surroundings. There was just him and a hard, grey boulder, which he must keep pushing.

The image blurred as he drifted out of unconsciousness. It was no good, he was awake again. He lay still, trying to clear the anxiety, but dark thoughts kept coming back. Perhaps he should attempt something new, think of pleasant things, his childhood? Yes, that would be good. How he wished he were back at home. Life was simpler back then, much easier than this complicated existence. He began to think of happy events during his childhood, it was working! Soon, he was fast asleep again.

The boulder looked small enough to hold, yet his outstretched hands barely reached around its craggy circumference. He made several attempts, his mind said it was possible, and yet…and yet…on and on…over and over…every attempt to gain control of the rock was futile.

Opening his eyes, he was restless, annoyed at being awake again. He tossed and turned in bed, but was determined to persevere, forcing himself to lie still. Almost immediately, his mind was back at home, memories of his childhood flooding in. But these thoughts only lasted a little while; worry over the next day was simply too great to ignore. He compelled himself to focus. Concentrate, man! Think of home! The storm of his mind calmed, and after a while, the darkness finally took him.

Running along a wide, open road. Alone in the desert, in the blistering heat. The sun was directly overhead, it must be noon. He had started running when it was dark; must have been running for hours. The loneliness was insufferable, despite the hundreds of people who had just appeared alongside him. Something was following. He could not see it, but felt it was somewhere near.

Suddenly, explosions, on the road behind. Ah, his reason for running: to escape the explosions. What was causing the explosions? He did not know. An explosion occurred beside him, then another, then one to the front. They must have been instigated by his pursuer; they had caught up with him. A flat, silvery-grey vessel flew overhead. It had no top, and appeared to be manned by several small, grey, impish creatures. Angry impish creatures, throwing grenade-like objects down onto the road below.

The shock of the attack woke him. This alternating between consciousness and unconsciousness was beginning to agitate him. But at least he was resting, getting some form of respite. Perhaps he might eventually fall into a deep sleep? He looked at the clock on the radio, three o'clock, three hours to go. Resting his head back on the pillow, he closed his eyes again. The cycle continued; he was back in the dream.

Bent on mayhem and destruction, the impish creatures had a look of determination, yet their missiles seemed to be having little effect. Explosions, yes, frightening explosions. But whether by design, or by lucky coincidence, they were missing the people below. Inciting fear must be their goal, and they were certainly succeeding with that. People were running, directionless and terrified. And yet…even that tactic was failing now. Realising the absence of any real danger, everyone had stopped running. They began to walk together, slowly, calmly. The silver vessel flew overhead, and explosions were still occurring, but there was no panic now.

The aircraft with the impish creatures eventually disappeared. Frustrated by their failure to terrorise, they had departed, off to frighten someone else. But wait. Everyone was running again. Was this a race? It must be. They were competing in a race, a marathon, perhaps? There were no spectators, no marshals, no barriers, no signage, no outriders to ensure everything went smoothly… nothing to indicate it was a race or marathon. They were just a group of people, running for no apparent reason.

His eyes opened. He looked at the clock. Four o'clock, two hours before his alarm. As he considered the next day's possible scenarios, he shuddered. A Common's statement; the press interrogation; revelations revealed; his character and reputation destroyed; police investigations; prosecution; court appearances; a guilty verdict; a prison sentence…the possibilities were too frightening to consider anymore. Sleep. He needed sleep.

Still running. Still with the multitude. It was getting dark. On and on, constantly running. They must have been running all day. The other runners slowly vanished into the distance. He was running alone.

Finally, he arrived at the large boulder, this time in the middle of the road. Under the heat of the blistering midday sun, he started pushing the boulder. It moved. Only slightly, but there was movement.

Night fell. He had managed to move the boulder a few inches. Stopping to take in his surroundings, the light from the moon illuminated what appeared to be trees further up the road. Looking across the vast expanse of desert, he could just make out the outline of a city in the distance.

Daylight: strolling slowly through the hustle and bustle of city streets; the people; the traffic; the noise of the city. A pedestrian crossing and a policeman, or cop, standing opposite, pointing, telling him not to cross. The policeman walked to the middle of the crossing. The traffic stopped, and the policeman beckoned. Safe to cross now.

He passed a stall selling hot dogs. It smelt delicious.

Still walking, now eating a fresh hot dog, he passed by a theatre: a play or a show perhaps? No, there was a bar down the road, much better.

Ice-chilled beer slipped down his dry throat. Another beer, this was more like it. Further down the bar, two men started quarrelling. The dispute escalated to an all-out fight; next the whole bar was fighting, time to exit.

Walking along the street, observing the scenes of the city. He saw two men drinking from bottles hidden in brown paper packaging, both sat watching the traffic between swigs. An attractive, scantily clad lady stood provocatively outside a bar. She was propositioning men, young and old, as they left or entered. An altercation: she was moved on by the bar manager, words of obscenities spilling from both parties as she walked down the street, to take her position outside another bar. A man staggered out of the second bar. A few words with the attractive lady; money exchanged hands. They started moving along the sidewalk, arm in arm.

The muffled sound of gun shots; a man rushed past. Women were screaming; men shouting; people dashing about. Sirens, police cars. Paramedics appeared, attending to two people lying on the ground. It was the same attractive woman who had been standing outside the bar, and the man she had walked off with. People were pointing and police started running in the same direction as the man who had just rushed by. Police drew their weapons; everyone stood back.

His body jerked upright in bed, cold sweat dripping down his neck. He was fretting again, the worry stronger than ever. Overwhelmed by a sense of helplessness, he settled back down, trying to relax. After a while, his weakness dissipated; he could start reasoning again.

Should he resign? Save the Party and Government any embarrassment? He could call the PM first thing and get it over with. Could he call him now? Perhaps not. The PM would not be best pleased about being woken at such an hour. What time was it anyway? He looked at the clock. Five a.m., only one hour to go. He could call him…get it over with…it would clear his mind and save a lot of trouble in the long run.

The more he thought about it, the more inviting the idea became. The newspapers had already gone to print, so it would only be the broadcast media to manage, and his department could easily handle television and radio with a simple press release. Of course, he would still have to deal with the committee and the planned interviews, but those would now only be formalities. He could give his side of the story; he had a better chance of controlling the damage with them than he had with the newspapers. Yes, there were options. He could work on it. But for now, he had best try and get some sleep. It might be easier now that he was feeling more positive.

A policeman was asking for witnesses, but everyone seemed oblivious to his request. The officer started talking into his radio. He heard the control room responding. Could not hear what was being said, except for an occasional beeping sound from the handset.

Every piece of conversation was followed by a beep. One beep…another beep…and another, longer this time.

'Good morning! It's six o'clock, and this is the Today programme, with John Humphreys and Nick Robinson. The main story this morning: Home Secretary, John Bartholomew, today faces questions from the Parliamentary Standards Committee regarding his alleged involvement with disgraced American financier, Carlos Montoya. We will be interviewing Mr Bartholomew at ten past eight, but first, here are the headlines, read by John Hedges.

'Before he was fatally gunned down outside a restaurant in New York City, Carlos Montoya was facing charges in relation to…'

Scrapbook of Memories

Having finished his morning coffee, Chadwick Banks, former top London barrister and QC, picked up the buff-coloured scrapbook of memories his daughter had left for him. It was the first time he had looked at it today. Pictures of family, friends, former colleagues…all there to help him, along with newspaper cuttings of some of his famous cases. Leafing through the pages, he sighed. There was nothing he recognised. A couple of newspaper cuttings, pages of photos, typed and hand-written notes…not one thing caught his attention. He was sure this was the book he had been looking at yesterday. But there was nothing, not even the faintest spark of a memory. He threw the book onto the bedside cabinet in frustration, putting his head back. Sometimes a five-minute snooze helped. Regroup and then try again. Five, perhaps ten, minutes later he picked up the book again. There, that was better, everything looked familiar now.

His once sharp memory was not what it used to be. Worse, with the muddled state of his mind, different memories had occasionally begun to merge, creating a quasi-reality which was challenging to manage, especially given his vivid imagination. He still had the intelligence to reason things through; could still do a thousand-piece jigsaw puzzle in record time, but when presented with this mixed-up reality he became perplexed and uncertain. He was trying. He was not a quitter and had never been the type to just give up, but when he tried too hard, he would get himself into a terrible state. Confusion led to frustration, and frustration led to despondency, at which point he resorted to taking his medication. It was the only thing that could completely calm the chaos.

The scrapbook. Some days it would jog a memory, other days it served no purpose. Despite the initial bad start, today looked like it was going to be a good day. Taking his daily perusal through the pictures and documents on show, carefully laid out in chronological order, he came across the letter offering him his first position in Chambers. Memories slowly drifted into his mind. He had probably seen it thousands of times, but like so much of the scrapbook's contents, it had not registered until today.

The letter soon triggered a whole host of long-suppressed memories and emotions. He remembered being over the moon. It had been his ambition to be counsel at one London's major law firms. Report to Head of Chambers on Tuesday the sixth of July, the letter had instructed him; details of his new position would be finalised then.

Putting the scrapbook down, he stared through the window at the Kent countryside, which surrounded the hospice he now called home. It was a long way from the hustle and bustle of London, the city where almost all his recollections were based.

It was late evening, during high summer, as he walked down a street overflowing with hotels. He noted the names as he passed: Beauchamp, Lancaster, Buckingham, Clarendon…nearly all of them converted Edwardian townhouses, with gleaming white walls and colourful window boxes. They were well-kept affairs, except for his, the Smart-Stay Hotel. There were obviously better to choose from, but instead, he had selected that one. The cheap price had been the overriding factor guiding his choice, but as it was only for three nights the shoddiness did not matter. Climbing the steps to the main entrance, he looked above the door: there was a faded, stained-glass window with the initials C.S. etched in the centre. Most likely, it dated back to when the hotel had been in its prime.

Despite the un-kempt look of the outside, the inside of the hotel was surprisingly pleasant. The young lady who checked him in was also pleasant enough, informing him, in her Eastern European accent, that the hotel no longer provided catering facilities, but that guests were welcome to use the dining area where there was a microwave and kettle.

After retrieving his key, he lugged his case and briefcase down the stairs to his basement room. That too seemed agreeable, and the specified en-suite facilities were in good working order. The only snag was that the single room he had booked turned out to be a triple: a divan and two wood-frame beds. The lady who had taken the reservation over the phone had seemed to struggle somewhat with English, so perhaps three nights had become three beds. Ah well, it was too late to make a fuss. Besides, there was a lot planned for the next day; all he really wanted was to curl up in bed and get a good night's sleep.

Staring out of the hospice window, it was winter outside — a sharp contrast to the evening summer sun, shining into the hotel room where his mind had returned once more. The light had been keeping him awake, it had taken him a while to drift off to sleep.

It was dark when he was suddenly woken by a knocking at the door. At first, he ignored it, but whoever was there seemed desperate and the knocking grew louder and more urgent. Using the light from an outside streetlamp, he looked at his watch. Three a.m. What was the emergency, he wondered? Perhaps there was a fire and the alarm system had failed? The thought panicked him; jumping out of bed, he reached for his dressing gown, quickly unlocking the door to find a young lady, barely more than a girl really, standing on the other side. Not the receptionist from earlier, but someone much shorter, wearing a blue pinafore dress, white apron, and bonnet. She was dressed more like a scullery maid from a period drama than an employee at a modern hotel.

At first, he thought it must be a stunt, pulled by former colleagues back home. They had arranged a stripper-gram and here she was, though this girl looked far too young to be a stripper, she was only in her early teens. She had been running and was finding it difficult to get her words out.

'H...h...here you are, Sir,' she gasped. 'Robinson sent me to look for you. Miss Peterson has arrived; she is waiting in the drawing room.'

'Robinson? Miss Peterson? You must have the wrong room, I've never heard of these people,' he mumbled, still half asleep. But the girl was adamant that he must come with her, to see this Miss Peterson.

'You must come, Sir. Miss Peterson was quite upset when we said we couldn't find you.'

Being disturbed in the middle of the night was bad enough, but not knowing who any of these people was making it even worse. But he had to go. It might be something important. What if something had happened at home? Or it could be an urgent message from Chambers? He made a point of looking at his watch.

'Okay,' he said. 'I'll come. But I hope this won't take too long. It's late, I'm tired, and I have a long day ahead of me tomorrow.'

Following the girl, he was astonished to find that his surroundings had changed entirely. His room had been one of several in the basement; in all probability, occupying the space where the kitchens and scullery had been back when the hotel was a townhouse. Looking around, the hotel rooms appeared to have disappeared, and a large, square room had taken their place. At least three people were busily preparing what looked to be a rather delightful meal.

His initial bewilderment slowly began to subside as he followed the girl up the stairs and into the main hotel area. When he had first arrived, he noted that the hotel had not been decorated for years, the furnishings a mishmash of ages and style. For instance, the desk in the reception had formerly been a church altar, and the dining area was constructed from an eclectic mix of tables and chairs. But now, as with the basement area, it had all changed: the wallpaper, the curtains, the floor…everything appeared to be exquisitely new, and all the furniture matched. They walked through the hotel dining area, which was now a drawing room; over a newly laid parquet floor in the hallway, which had previously been carpeted, to the bottom of the main staircase.

He realised that he was no longer in the hotel, but in the same building at a much earlier time. When exactly was difficult to determine, but there were a few clues: the electric lighting looked fairly modern, so it must be the twentieth century, and the black and white television, sitting in what had been the reception area, dated back to the 1950s. Considering the newness of the household furnishings, he could assume the owners of the house would have made a point to purchase the most recent television set, thus the current date must be sometime during the 1950s.

A sense of déjà vu hit him, as he followed the girl up the stairs and into another expensively furnished room. He was certain he had been there before, and could instinctively predict what going to happen next, despite not being entirely sure what was happening or even where he was. The people depicted in the pictures on the walls seemed vaguely familiar, as did the attractive young lady who smiled sweetly as he entered the room. He could smell her sweet perfume, and hear the rustle of her chiffon dress, as she reached to put her arms around him.

'Where have you been?' she asked, before kissing him on the lips. 'You weren't at the meeting this afternoon and Daddy's not best pleased. He says that if you continue like this you'll be out of the company.' She sighed deeply, 'And the marriage will be off, our marriage!'

It was like a scene from a Victorian melodrama. Undoubtedly, this was the Miss Peterson who had been waiting for him, and assumedly they know each other, well enough to be getting married. Yet he did not know her first name, let alone how they had met, or indeed anything about their supposed relationship. He searched desperately for something to say, something constructive, something that might help to answer one of the hundreds of questions running through his mind. What was happening? Why had he gone back in time, to the 1950s? Who was the girl who had led him here? What company was Miss Peterson referring to; the meeting he was supposed to have attended? And who was Daddy? More importantly, was he even himself, or was he currently reliving someone else's life?

Perplexity dragged him out of his daydream. Still staring out of the hospice window, his mind was in a state of confusion. Meeting Daddy? Ah, his meeting with the Head of Chambers the next day, perhaps the Head was her father? Anxiety was creeping in. As had happened all too frequently over the past few months, the thoughts running through his mind were impossibly confusing. He reached for his medication. No. Stop. He could fight it. He would fight it. He gathered his resolve, taking deep breaths just as the doctor had told him to. A deep breath cleared his mind, a little. He had to go with the flow and play along. Go with the flow and play along. He repeated this mantra to himself. Sooner or later, everything would become apparent, he was sure of it.

Another deep breath followed by another. One more. Slowly, his mind relaxed, enough to reason the situation. He was daydreaming; reliving a moment in the past where he had imagined himself as someone else. Or was he? Had it been his imagination, or had he really been this person, once upon a time? Confusion again. Was this his house, or someone else's? He was helplessly out of his depth.

'Calm down,' he whispered to himself. 'Relive the experience.'

He was back in the room with Miss Peterson. It was so strange, everyone seemed to know him. If only he could reciprocate. He put on a thoughtful expression, stalling for time, giving himself a moment to think. Finally, he decided to tell Miss Peterson the truth, or at least a truth of sorts.

'I was travelling,' he answered, as his excuse for supposedly not attending the meeting with her father.

Her brown eyes widened, and she grabbed hold of his shoulders, shaking him in frustration.

'Travelling? Travelling? When you knew full well you had an important meeting with Daddy, and the rest of the Board?' She sighed deeply, shaking her head incredulously. 'What on earth were you thinking? You had better start making more of an effort, or I swear it will all be over!'

'What will be over?' he enquired in a firm but soothing voice, attempting to coax some information out of her whilst also trying to calm her temper. Unfortunately, his efforts had the opposite effect, only fuelling her frustration.

'You know exactly what I mean,' she screamed at him, on the verge of tears.

She was almost incandescent with rage, and he could sense the girl who had guided him earlier becoming increasingly alarmed at the strained atmosphere.

'Would Sir and Miss like some tea?' she asked quietly, trying to defuse the situation.

'What an excellent idea! Yes, tea, we should have tea,' he replied enthusiastically, thankful for the timely intervention. 'I'm sure Miss Peterson would like some tea? Thank you, err—'

'Janet, Sir,' prompted the girl, obviously surprised that he had forgotten her name.

'Janet, yes, that's right. How could I forget? Thank you, Janet, tea would be lovely.'

'Very good, Sir.' Janet curtsied to him, then repeated the curtsy to Miss Peterson. 'Miss Peterson? Tea?'

'Oh, Janet, I have told you before, please call me Veronica. I refuse to stand on ceremony, not like your so-called master here. He thinks he is something special, but really, he is as common as we are. Just likes to splash his money around.'

A broad grin appeared on Janet's face.

'Yes, Miss Peterson,' she replied, before remembering what she had just been told. 'Sorry, Miss Veronica.'

Then she turned, threw a sarcastic 'Sir' in his direction, and left the room with a smirk. It was starting to make sense now. The girl, who he assumed was a servant of some kind, was called Janet, and the woman was his fiancée, Miss Veronica Peterson. He turned to Veronica.

'Shall we talk about this over some tea?' he suggested, beckoning her to a chaise longue which sat beneath the painting of some great sea lord. Veronica nodded curtly, but as soon as they were seated, she began to complain.

'I have had it with you and your 'tea, tea, tea'. All you ever say is 'why don't we drink some tea; everything will be fine'. Enough is enough. I want answers—'

If he was currently reliving the life of this other person, he desperately hoped that Veronica would say his name soon. At least then he would know who he was supposed to be. After all, if he were to ask her outright, he would almost certainly be perceived as insane, or she would assume that he was playing some silly game with her, which judging by her present uncompromising mood would not go down well. So he sat, silently, waiting, and after a few moments of contemplation, she was calm enough to continue.

'And do you know what else frustrates me? You and your bloody writing, with your bloody writing friends. You're becoming exactly like them. They don't live in the real world, but you do…' her voice softened as she leant in closer. 'But you do, and if you become any more like them, you'll lose everything: my father's respect, the business partnership, everything…even me.'

The picture was clearing. He was a writer, a considerably wealthy one at that, and was about to marry into a family with strong business connections. He looked up from his musings to see that Janet had arrived with the tea, and immediately took charge of the situation, feeling more confident in his position now that he had accumulated this new knowledge.

'Thank you, Janet, just leave it on the side there,' he requested, firmly but politely. Looking up at the clock on the mantel piece, he noticed that it was no longer three a.m. but almost half-past seven in the evening. 'Why don't you take the rest of the evening off? I can manage now.' He suddenly remembered the meal he had seen being prepared downstairs. 'And could you tell the others that they can go too when they have finished? I'm sure I can cope with dishing up a couple of plates. I'm common enough,' he smiled, winking at Veronica. To his relief, his comment was successful, and Veronica looked happy for the first time since he had arrived.

'Yes, Janet, we can manage from here. Thank you,' Veronica added with a smile. Janet smiled back, obviously relieved that the tension had eased and happy to see her master in such a good mood.

'Goodnight then, Miss. Sir,' replied Janet, bobbing a curtsy to them both before scampering out of the door. As soon as she had disappeared, Veronica snuggled up to him.

'You are such a softy,' she murmured, as he put his arms around her. 'You have never given the servants a night off before...are you doing all this just to please me?'

Images of Veronica and the room began to dissolve, and his eyes focused once more on the letter in the scrapbook. He thought of the next day, and the meeting with the Head of Chambers.

He was back in of the offices at Chambers, with the practice secretary, or administrator, whatever her role was. Her name had escaped him. He should remember this. He had worked with her for the best part of fifteen years. What was her name? His mind was blank. He took a deep breath, trying to relax. It would come eventually, he just needed to focus his mind on something else for a moment. He took another deep breath and his mind cleared. Suddenly he remembered. Natasha. That was it, Natasha. Of course.

Her voice began to echo through his mind.

'Wow, that was some dream!' she exclaimed, sorting through a pile of unopened post. 'I've got to know what happened next: did she stay for dinner?' Her eyes widened in expectation. 'Wait, did she stay the night?'

'Sorry, I'm far too much of a gentleman to divulge any more details.'

'Ugh, spoil-sport. Alone in the house with an attractive young lady, who also happened to be your fiancée?' Her face hardened. 'I want details. Come on, the full works.'

'Sorry, but no. In any case, to be honest with you, I can't really remember.'

'Aw! But I was looking forward to the rest.'

'Me too,' he laughed. 'She was a stunner. It would have certainly been interesting.'

'I bet. Ooh describe her to me! I bet she had big—'

'Now, come on,' he said, holding his hand out to stop her. 'I've told you already, I'm too much of a gentleman. It was a shame though. I was hoping to find out more; explore the rest of the house; see what the hotel looked like all those years before…and, of course, learn more about me and this Veronica Peterson: the business, the writing, the marriage and all that…even just to see what I looked like would have been nice.'

He thought of Natasha. Ah Natasha, she was as beautiful now as she had been back then. A slim, blonde twenty-year-old, with a bubbly personality and a vivid, playful, often lewd imagination. He was going to enjoy this.

Looking down at her watch, Natasha sighed, 'I haven't a clue where the Head of Chambers is, he should be here by now.'

'Perhaps he had to go to court?'

'Nah, he has nothing until Thursday. If he doesn't turn up soon, I'll give you a list of pubs to try. It's not the first time he has forgotten a meeting. Not so long ago he forgot about a court appearance; the judge had to suspend the hearing until we found him, drinking in a pub in Holborn.'

'He likes a drink, then? A man after my own heart. How about you? I am sure a young lady like yourself must enjoy a drink now and again? Perhaps we could—'

Now it was she who held up her hand. 'Mr Banks, before we start working together, I should emphasise that our relationship must remain strictly formal. We can only work together if —' She was wearing a low-cut top, and on seeing him staring at her cleavage, pushed her shoulders back. Her chest moved forward to meet his gaze. 'But I don't mind the occasional flirt, it never hurts, and it does brighten up the day, doesn't it?'

'Of course, we must be professional. I am a married man, so—' He was about to continue when the rather inebriated Head of Chambers burst into the room, apologising for his lateness. After introductions had been made, his new superior gave him an impressively vice-like handshake.

'Welcome to the company, Banks. I am sure you will soon settle in with us. Now, to business.'

The meeting was illuminating, to the point where he started doubting whether he should take the position at all. It seemed his predecessor had been a workaholic, and he was expected to behave likewise.

'Oh, did I mention? You will also be overseeing next year's intake of trainees,' added the Head, halfway through the meeting.

'Actually, you didn't, no. Indeed, Counsel was the position I applied for, but am I now to understand that my new role will be a Senior Counsel position? With several outstanding cases to manage, difficult cases at that, not to mention the responsibility of overseeing half a dozen juniors? Forgive me, but I don't think I caught any of this at the first interview.'

'So sorry, your predecessor did rather leave us in the lurch. He left very suddenly, you understand?'

Oh, I wonder why, he thought sarcastically to himself.

'Of course, we don't want you to feel pressured. If you need help with anything, please just say the word. You will find that everyone knows their job, so you can basically leave them to get on with it.'

'I am relieved to hear it. But what about the trainees?'

'Oh, don't worry about them. They shouldn't be any hassle. I have arranged for them to come during the first week of August. You know the drill: induction, showing them around and all that. I am sure you'll be fine making the arrangements.'

'Know the drill? I hardly know the Chambers myself, that's why I'm here today.'

'Not to worry. Natasha knows what to do. Ask her nicely and I'm sure she will be more than willing to help.'

'That's nice to know. What else can Natasha do?'

'She's a lovely girl, isn't she? Only just recently started herself. Totally brilliant, a whiz when it comes to organising things, you'll love her. Not in the literal sense, of course.'

'I'm sure she will be a great help. And she seems pleasant enough.'

'Did she mention her partner?'

'No.'

'Ah, yes, well…she bats for the other side if you know what I mean. Currently dating one of the junior secretaries. Probably not my place to say really, but I think they're planning to move in together.'

'Well, thanks for letting me know. Probably for the best. After all, I wouldn't want to make a fool of myself.'

'Quite…quite…how long did you say you were staying in London?'

'A couple of days. There's a lot to sort out, mostly living arrangements. I'll rent a flat for the first few months while I look for something more permanent. Then my wife will join me down here.'

'Jolly good. Well, Natasha will be in tomorrow.'

'Fantastic, tomorrow then.'

Later that afternoon, he was wandering along a street. He had hoped to be sorting out his accommodation, but that would have to wait until tomorrow. Lunch with the Head of Chambers had been a boozy affair, in one of the backstreet pubs next to the Inns of Court. He had not consumed such a vast volume of alcohol in a long time, and as a consequence he was in no fit state to do anything constructive. Instead, he decided to explore his new surroundings.

His plan was to travel back home to Manchester most weekends, so he decided to check the route from Chambers to Euston, to see whether he could feasibly catch the train straight after work on a Friday. Utilising the A to Z he had purchased from WHSmith the day before, it only took a quick scan of the route and his surroundings before he was on his way again. He considered backtracking down Euston Road to the British Library; there was always an exhibition on there, it would be something to do…no. It would be too intellectual. He didn't have the focus for that right now, and besides, he still had a long afternoon ahead of him.

Lunching with the Head had stimulated his taste for alcohol, so he decided to give the Library a miss and head towards Tottenham Court Road. His future boss had suggested several hostelries along that road that were worth trying, insisting that if he was going to work in London, he needed to learn the pubs.

Going past Warren Street, and the Tube station of the same name, a feeling of déjà vu came over him, similar to the feeling he had experienced at the hotel the night before. This was his first time in this part of London, yet he felt certain he had been here before. The déjà vu grew stronger about one hundred yards or so later, when he arrived outside the Mortimer's Cross, the first of the Head's recommendations. The feeling grew stronger still when he came to The Half Moon, a five-minute walk away from the Mortimer's Cross, on the opposite side of the road. The striking Victorian gothic architecture and large windows, sweeping round into a side street, seemed familiar, and as he entered the pub, he realised the same was true of the interior décor. He knew this place.

'Afternoon, love, what can I get you?' asked a middle-aged barmaid, busy loading freshly washed glasses onto a shelf beneath the bar.

He had been drinking Fosters all day, so he asked for more of the same.

'Gorgeous day,' he added casually, trying to make small talk.

'It really is,' replied the barmaid, having found a suitably branded Fosters glass. 'It's about time we started having some decent summer weather, hasn't it been awful lately?'

'You can say that again,' he said, scanning the pub to see who else was in. Apart from the three sat outside – a girl and two lads – there was a young couple sitting by one of the front windows and several individuals dotted around the pub, most of them smoking and reading newspapers. 'Quiet today,' he continued.

'It is now,' answered the barmaid, concentrating on his drink. 'It was busier at lunchtime, with the office workers, and will be busy again later when they've all finished for the day. But this is a quiet time of year for us, what with all the students gone for the summer. It gets pretty dead, especially in the evenings. The gaffer was talking about closing early some nights, but I'm hoping he'll change his mind, I need the money.'

'I hope he does change his mind, it's a nice pub, and the quiet makes a pleasant change. I can imagine it gets very busy when all the students are around.' He was still scanning the room, trying to understand why everything looked so familiar, as the barmaid finished pouring his pint and placed it on the counter.

'It was all done out a couple of months ago,' she told him, gesturing to the far end of the pub. 'And we had the bottom end converted into a dining area. Two twenty please, love.'

'Thanks,' he replied, handing over a few coins from his pocket.

'So, what brings you up to London, then? I can tell you're not a local.'

'I've just been appointed to one of the local Chambers, so I thought I'd spend the afternoon checking out the area.'

'Chambers? I'll be going there in September, I've got a placement,' piped up a voice behind him. Turning round, he saw a girl walking towards him with a handful of empty glasses. He recognised her as one of the three who had been sitting outside.

'Yes, Mel,' laughed the woman behind the bar. 'We know, you haven't stopped talking about it since Friday.'

'But I'm so excited!' exclaimed the girl, hurriedly placing the glasses on top of the bar, ready for cleaning.

He could feel her penetrating stare as she looked towards him.

'I have been a bit worried though,' she said quietly, with a concerned look on her face. 'Will they accept me with my hair like this? I can change it if I need to.' She ran her fingers through her mop of short, white hair. 'I mean, when I went for the interview, I was my natural brown, but now I've changed it—' She smiled. 'What with it being a posh place and all that…'

He had taken an instant liking to this girl. Her infectious smile drew him in, and he admired her respect: he had never met a prospective junior member who had considered whether their appearance was appropriate, and was so willing to change what they looked like to ensure they fit in. Usually, the juniors had to be told, often multiple times. Stepping forward, he pretended to scrutinise her hair.

'Hmm, let me see now…' he said in his most serious voice. 'Bleached with green streaks…' She appeared so worried by his tone that he almost laughed aloud, but he restrained himself, settling for a soft smile instead. 'Don't worry, you'll be absolutely fine. And if anyone says anything, you tell them that Mr Banks of Doverdale and Tomlinson gave you his personal approval.' The girl grinned, rushing forward, and hugging him tightly.

'Aww, you're so sweet! I could kiss you!'

If he were honest with himself, he would not have minded if she had kissed him. Despite her punk appearance, or perhaps because of her punk appearance, along with her nose stud and eye piercings, he found her agreeably eye-catching. About his height and slightly skinny, though not skinny enough to worry about, she was just his type of girl, if he had been twenty years younger. He sighed to himself. He must resist this temptation. After all, he was married. The thought changed nothing; just standing next to her aroused his excitement. She was obviously popular, even the few customers who had overheard their conversation were smiling. No. He must resist. Shame, though, she was gorgeous. Still, he could always fantasise over what might have been. He envied all the lads her own age she must have fawning after her, lucky blighters.

'How about piercings?' she asked, concerned again. 'I can take them out when I start, but I would really rather leave them in.'

He was stunned, was she serious, or was she just joking now? Might as well play along, he thought to himself. No harm in a flirt.

'Well, it depends,' he said, again in his serious voice. 'Are there any more piercings about your person? I will, of course, have to inspect them if so. There are strict rules, you know.'

She glanced up at him, catching the flirtatious look in his eye. Smiling shyly, she ran her tongue over her lips.

'One or two. I can show you if you like. Just say when,' she smirked, winking at him. It was obvious that she was enjoying this game. God, she was really testing his resolve.

'Now, for that I can't wait,' he replied, and the girl laughed delightedly in response.

'Neither can I,' she said, running her hand provocatively over her body. 'I'll look forward to your little inspection.'

Thoughts of her intimate piercings and touching her naked body only heightened his excitement. Staring at her, mentally undressing her, he was lost in thought.

'Melanie!' shouted the older barmaid, shocking him out of his fantasies. 'Dave's here now,' she gestured towards the young man who had just entered the pub. 'Why don't you go for your break now?'

'Dave!' squealed the girl, looking in the direction of the young man. She turned back to look at him, caressing his arm with the back of her hand. 'It was nice to meet you, I'm sure we'll be seeing a lot more of each other, if our Chambers are nearby.' He was unsure what she meant exactly by 'seeing a lot more', but her hand on his arm and the shiver of anticipation it had triggered made him hopeful. 'And of course, you'll have to inspect my piercings some time, make sure they all comply to those strict rules of yours,' she added, with a mischievous grin.

'I'll look forward to it,' he laughed, before she turned and began to walk towards Dave. But before she reached the young man she stopped suddenly, running back towards him, and kissing him firmly on the lips.

'Bye for now,' she whispered softly, before racing back towards Dave again.

'Sorry about that,' sighed the older barmaid. 'Mel can be quite a handful.'

'She certainly can,' he replied, trying to make the taste of her kiss last for as long as possible. They both watched as Melanie shared a passionate kiss with Dave, and he felt a pang of jealousy as they walked out into the street, hand in hand. 'I take it that's her boyfriend?'

'Yeah, that's Dave, probably the best guy she's ever had. She normally attracts the rough ones, but Dave's nice. She really needs someone to look after her, a guide if you like. You've seen what she's like, I just hope she doesn't mix with the wrong crowd after she's left here. She might look confident, but deep down she's vulnerable and easily led.'

'I'm sure she'll be fine once she's settled into her new job, they will look after her. At least she's staying local, so her friends will still be around. It's not like she's going hundreds of miles from home to another town.'

'I hope you're right.'

He continued to reassure the barmaid as she poured him another drink. While it was being prepared, he turned to make for the toilet, but after walking only a few yards he found himself at the entrance to the kitchens. On returning, the barmaid was waiting with his drink. He could have sworn he had chosen the correct route.

'Sorry, this is embarrassing, but you couldn't tell me where the toilets are could you?' he asked apologetically. 'Seems I went in the wrong direction.'

She laughed kindly. 'I wondered where you'd wandered off to, thought I'd lost you.' She pointed to a door next to the front window, opposite the main entrance. 'Through that door and up the stairs. They're at the top.'

'For some reason I thought they were down there,' he said, signalling in the direction from which he had just come. The barmaid nodded her head in the same direction.

'Funny you should say that. They used to be down there, until we started doing food. That's when we moved them upstairs.'

Placing the scrapbook on the table next to him, he pressed his head into the back of the chair and closed his eyes. Other than the occasional muffled voices outside his room, the only sound was the ticking of the clock on the wall. His thoughts were haphazard, alternating between past and present, the quietness of the hospice's country setting a welcome respite from the noise of the city.

His mind was a cloud of numbness as he made his way down Tottenham Court Road, the extra pints in The Half Moon having chased away all his worries and cares. He ambled along to where Tottenham Court Road met Oxford Street, then crossed the junction to the Centre Point tower block, before turning around ready for the long walk back towards Warren Street and Euston Road.

Most of the shop frontages were of modern design, with large glass windows, and many were displaying hi-tech sound and video equipment. There were a few, however, that appeared to him in black and white, and seemed to be from a different age entirely. Even the people and motor vehicles surrounding them appeared to be from an earlier time. His view of the street constantly alternated between old time scenes, usually found in nostalgic picture books, and modern-day London.

Old, black and white…modern, colour…old, black and white…modern, colour…back and forth until he arrived at Goodge Street Tube Station. Modern, colour…but, this time, it remained that way. A little further on, he turned left in to a side street, then ambled down to where The Sun stood on the junction with another street. Not one of the Head's recommended pubs, but it was worth a try. The colourful hanging baskets were effective at distracting the eye from the rest of the building which, like his hotel, looked tired and run-down. Inside it was much the same; the furnishings looked clean but had clearly not been updated for many years. The woman behind the bar was replenishing the drinks cabinet. Must have been a busy lunchtime, he thought to himself. Clearly it was a popular pub, despite the outdated furnishings.

'You okay there?' the woman asked, without looking up.

He responded politely, ordering himself a drink, and after a few words of small talk he took his drink and settled down on one of the long bench seats, beneath the window next to the entrance. Pulling a newspaper from his case, he started to read, but the warm afternoon sun on his back made him sleepy. The words blurred, and a short while later he fell fast asleep.

The next thing he knew, he was being rudely awakened by an insistent voice.

'I know you, Charles Smart, yes? Charles, where have you been all this time? It's me, John, remember?' He twisted his head, and with half open eyes he saw an elderly gentleman standing over him. Wearing an old, dishevelled suit, the old man must have just arrived, for until that moment it had been just the barmaid and himself in the pub. The man leant forward, squinting as he examined him.

'Yes, it is you! So nice to see you, Charles.'

'I'm sorry, you must be mistaken, my name's not Charles Smart, and I've definitely never been here before, not to this part of London anyway.'

'Come on, Charles, nonsense! I know you too well, always been a bit on the illusive side. What are you up to this time?'

'I'm sorry, but my name's not Charles Smart. It's Banks.'

Without an invitation, the old man sat down alongside him, placing his drink on the small round table in front of them. Despite still feeling groggy, he was intrigued by this old man, and the man's adamance that he was someone called Charles Smart. Perhaps he had a body double? No, that was unlikely. The old man had probably mistaken him for someone else, after all, the man's eyesight was clearly failing. That said, he had still managed to find the seat and table without too much difficulty. Perhaps the stranger's memory was also failing? Working in the legal profession, he had learnt that memories often changed as people grew older.

Despite these very logical explanations, he could not curb his curiosity, and decided to continue probing the old man for details.

'He does sound like a rather interesting fellow though, this Charles Smart. Why don't you tell me a little more about him, John?

The old man looked at him and grinned broadly, having clearly taken the question as a joke.

'You still selling cars, Charles? I know you went in for the quality stuff: Rollers, Bentleys, and the like. You made a tidy packet if I remember right, probably more than the rest of us put together. You had quite a business going, until you decided to pack it all in and take up writing.'

Interesting. The previous evening, Veronica Peterson had referred to his writing, and how it had taken precedence over his business interests. The coincidence seemed uncanny…questioning this old man might answer some of his questions regarding last night's meeting with Miss Peterson. This old man was under the impression that his name was Charles Smart, and was refusing to accept otherwise...perhaps Charles Smart held the key to this mystery? He decided to play along; pretend to be Charles Smart; see what he could uncover.

'I am sorry, John, I just can't quite remember...when did we meet again? I've been away a long time.'

'Don't you remember? I had the pitch next to you in Warren Street. I know the rest of us were only selling cheaper family motors but—'

The mention of Warren Street suddenly jogged his memory.

'That's right,' he interjected. 'We were bloody good, weren't we? Shifted loads of motors...' He paused, hoping the old man would go further.

'The best, no one could touch us.'

'Yes. Yes, I remember now.' He thought of what Veronica had said, something about him going into partnership with her father. 'I went into business with Peterson, didn't I?'

'You did, but only so you could get your hands on old man Peterson's daughter. She was a stunner, wasn't she?'

'She was something,' he replied, thinking of how attractive Veronica was.

'You can say that again. Everyone on the strip was after her, and not only because she was gorgeous. Wanted to get in with her old man, didn't they? And you managed it, lucky sod. Got both. Until you decided to chuck it all in.' The old man sighed heavily and stared at him. 'Had that hare-brained idea that you wanted to be a writer. You still writing?'

A picture was forming. In this strange, alternate life, his name was Charles Smart, he sold expensive cars in Warren Street, and was about to marry the daughter of one of the biggest car dealers in the area. But there were gaps in the story. What had happened between himself and Veronica? What of the partnership? His career as a writer? His life before becoming a car dealer?

'Yes, still writing,' he replied. He decided to take a gamble, hoping his new acquaintance would call him out if he was wrong. 'I thought you knew? I have had several books published.'

The gamble was lost on the old man. 'Well, you know I was never one for reading. Never even read a newspaper. Cars were my life.' John paused. 'Haven't seen you since you stopped dealing, it's good to hear you're doing alright for yourself.'

He felt a sudden urge to apologise to this old man for his alter ego's lack of courtesy, leaving without a word and apparently cutting him off entirely. It was just not right; they had been fellow car dealers after all. 'A little late now to say sorry, but I hope you managed by yourself?'

'Ah, don't worry, bygones are bygones. Anyway, I got by until the council moved us on. Smarten up the area they said, then came up with this fancy new name for the place, Fitzrovia, or something like that.'

'I remember reading about it. When was that now? I can't quite remember.'

'About '59 or '60 wasn't it? It's all in the past now, but I remember the motors we shifted.'

They were going round in circles. He decided to change tack entirely. 'I thought you would have bought one those wartime bomb sites; they've all been turned into car lots haven't they?'

The old man took a moment to compose his answer. 'I thought about it, but decided it wasn't for me, owning a pitch and all that. Not the same as wheeling and dealing on the street, or in the pub like we did, so I decided to chuck it all in.'

'Sorry to hear that. What did you do?'

'Worked for the council. It was only a few years until retirement. They got me working on the bins.'

'Bet you noticed the change, selling cars then all that heavy lifting? Those metal bins weigh a ton.'

'It was tough to begin with, but then again, it was a lot more reliable than dealing. The regular wage packet more than made up for the heavy lumber. But what about you, did you stay with Veronica?'

So, as Charles Smart, he evidently had married Veronica Peterson, or at least they had stayed together. He was stumped as to what reply to give, so he made something up. 'Yes, we did stay together—' He suddenly thought of what Veronica had said about his writing friends. 'That is, until she ran off with one of my writing colleagues.'

The old man gave him a consoling look. 'Women, eh? You can never trust them.'

He looked over at the old man's glass. It was almost empty. 'Another pint?' he asked, pointing to the glass.

The old man laughed. 'I thought you'd never ask! But then, you were always tight when it came to your round.' John nodded towards the bar. 'Tracey knows what I'm drinking.'

At the bar, he asked for another pint of whatever John was drinking.

The barmaid stared at him. 'Sorry,' she said, her face full of confusion. 'John? Who's John?'

'John, he's sat—' he looked across to where he had been sitting, but the long bench seat was empty. The old man had disappeared; a quarter-full glass of beer, his own beer, was the only thing left on the table.

'I could have sworn I was just speaking to an old chap. John, he said his name was.'

'I'm sorry,' repeated the barmaid. 'You're the only one who's been in, and you've been asleep for the past half hour. Looked so peaceful too, you must have been exhausted.'

'Who was this John then?' he wondered, out loud.

The barmaid looked puzzled. 'Well, there was this old chap who used to sit in that same seat you've been sitting in. Sat on that bench every day without fail, for years. We used to call it John's Corner, perhaps you saw the plaque on the wall and that's where you got the name from?' She shook her head sadly. 'He passed away a few months back, that's when we put the plaque up.'

He had failed to notice it before, but as he looked across at the bench, he spotted the brass plaque, screwed to the wall. As his pint was almost finished anyway, he asked for another, walking across to inspect the plaque as he waited for the barmaid to pour his drink.

John's Corner

A friend forever in our memories, The Sun.

He walked back to the bar. 'Do you know any more about this John?' he asked.

'Well, we knew him from when he worked for the council, on the bins. But he always used to talk about the good old days when he sold cars. In Warren Street, I think it was, just up the road there,' she added, pointing vaguely in that direction. 'Course, none of us are old enough to remember that. But, according to him, he had quite a business going.'

'And Smart, Charles Smart?'

'Yes, he would occasionally mention him. They had pitches next to each other apparently. How did you know that name?'

He paused briefly, trying to come up with a plausible explanation. 'Umm…I heard his name a couple of days ago, in another context. A writer from Bedford Place, if I remember correctly, who was also in the motor business.'

'That sounds like him. Most nights we have a couple of local historians in, they could probably tell you more about it, if you're interested?'

'Thanks, I might come back later,' he replied, before returning to the table with his drink.

A knock at the door jolted him back to reality. A young nurse entered the room, and he instantly recognised her blue uniform. 'Hello, Janet, are you here to tell me that Miss Peterson has arrived?'

'No, Mr. Banks. I'm here to give your medication, and to remind you that your daughter, Natasha, will be here shortly.' She smiled. 'You got my name right though, well done.'

He was searching his memory. 'Natasha? Doesn't she work—'

'Yes, your daughter, Natasha, remember?'

He was very confused but agreed anyway. She spoke with such certainty, and he could think of no reason not to believe her. 'Oh yes, that's right.'

Running her fingers through her hair, which was bleached with green streaks, Janet searched the room with her eyes. 'Ah, here it is,' she said, lifting a buff-coloured folder from the dresser. 'I left it last night: something to read while I sat in with you. You were having a restless night.'

'Was I?' He could not remember falling asleep in the first place.

'Yeah, it gave me the chance to catch up on my notes.'

'Well, it certainly looks interesting,' he added, trying to show interest.

'It is. It's for my college assignment. I'm looking at car dealers who worked in the streets around Bloomsbury, before and after the Second World War. I thought it would be boring, at first, but it's fascinating once you start researching. Seems it was quite a business, with some really colourful characters. Proper wheeler-dealers they were,' she said, smiling at the pun.

He smiled back. 'It definitely sounds an interesting subject.'

'It is. I thought you might have picked it up, I know how inquisitive you are. Plus, it's almost the same colour as your scrapbook.'

'Is it? They don't look at all similar to me. And I've been looking though that scrapbook a lot recently.'

'Oh, it's really good, isn't it? Such a lovely idea. I bet it brings back lots of memories.'

'Yes…I've been revisiting a trip I made to London, many years ago.' He held up the page displaying the letter. 'It's amazing how a simple letter can take you back.'

'Your daughter's done such a good job, putting it all together. You must be really proud.'

'Natasha…yes…yes, I am, so proud.'

'She's an angel. She'll be here to see you shortly, anyway, so you can tell her all about your trip. If you like, I can leave my folder for you to look at. It's only bits and pieces, but I'm sure you'll find it interesting. In fact, you might find you know something about it, having been in the legal profession yourself, and in roughly the same part of London as well.'

'Yes, that would be nice, thank you. I've been looking through the scrapbook this morning.'

'That's great.' Janet glanced at the clock. 'Sorry, but I must get on, loads to do as usual.' She waited a moment while he took his medication, to make sure he had taken it, then swiftly left the room.

As soon as Janet had left, he picked up her folder. Inside was a mass of photocopies, hand-written notes, and two newspaper articles. It was these two cuttings that caught his eye.

Petersons Smart Move

Petersons, the car people, have announced their merger with Smart, the prestigious car dealer. All things considered, it appears to be more a marriage of convenience than anything else. Petersons will be providing the showrooms while Smart will be bringing his expertise, and wealthy clients. But will the marriage last, with their two completely different modes of operation? Though they both started out selling cars on the side of the road, next to London's Euston Station, this is where the similarity ends. David Peterson went on to build a network of branches throughout London and the Home Counties, unlike Charles Smart, who is a throwback to the war-time spivs, making his money doing deals on the street or in the pub. He has never gone in for showrooms, simply building his multimillion-pound business through word of mouth.

There are also their differing personalities to consider. Peterson is known to be a shrewd businessman, driving hard bargains with major motor manufactures. Smart, on the other hand, is an eccentric who recently made a name for himself through his writing. He has already been signed by a major publisher, and whether his heart remains loyal to cars remains to be seen. Peterson's may end up being lumbered with just a handful of wealthy clients, and no one to develop that side of the business.

Daily Telegraph, May 1952

A Smart Quandary

Last week, we discussed the sudden death of the maverick car dealer and bestselling author, Charles Smart. Now, his ex-wife, Veronica Smart née Peterson, is at a loss as to what to do with her former husband's home in Bedford Place. She is already heiress to her father's lucrative motor company, not to mention Smart's shares in the company, which were sold to Peterson as part of his daughter's marriage settlement. Given that her former husband left no apparent successor, the settlement of their divorce means she now stands to benefit from all his assets. While the rights to Smart's literary works are already worth a tidy sum, the question remains: what to do with the house in Bloomsbury, worth just shy of one million pounds?

Close sources have informed the Diary that her father is planning to cash in on London's growing tourist market by opening a chain of hotels. Could the first be in Bedford Place? Several houses in the area have already succumbed to hotel

chains…could a new Peterson-Smart
Hotel be next? Watch this space.
'Londoner's Diary'

London Evening Standard, November 1958

Snakes and Ladders

I

There was a nasty chill to the air that night. But for Adam, the tea was warm and the atmosphere congenial, as he talked with Evelyn in the lounge of her rented town house. They worked in the same office together and had been dating for just over a month. It had started with small talk over the computers, then breaks spent together, before he had eventually summoned up the courage to ask her out. After that, they had visited art galleries and museums, been out for a few meals, spent evenings at the cinema…the things people usually did when they started dating. But this was the first time she had invited him back to her house after a night out.

They were in the middle of discussing the latest *Lord of the Rings* film, which they had just been to see, when Evelyn suddenly asked if he wanted to go upstairs.

'I can take you to somewhere fantastic. It'll blow your mind,' she said.

He nearly choked on his tea at the suggestion. This was not quite what he had been expecting, not just yet anyway. He already considered himself lucky, he was dating his perfect fantasy. They shared the same interests: The *Lord of the Rings* franchise; *Dungeons and Dragons*; sci-fi and fantasy games. Plus, she was nothing like the other girls in the office. With her jet-black hair, black t-shirts, and dark, faded jeans she looked the perfect goth.

Evelyn had already dated a couple of his colleagues, who had both confided in him about how strange and mysterious she was. She was just as they had expected her to be. Her 'weirdness' was the talk of the office and she elicited curiosity; it was obvious that his colleagues had only dated her to see what she was really like, and to find out what it was like to have sex with a goth. Unfortunately for them, she must have realised their game, and despite their attempts to charm her neither of them had ever been invited into her house, let alone her bedroom, after a night out. One of his colleagues had been so put out by her rejection that he had vindictively suggested she was a closet lesbian, who only dated men to cover up her real preferences.

Regardless of how she really felt, Adam felt he must have been someone special that night. Here he was, being asked to join her in her bedroom, the place where apparently few, if any, men had visited.

'Are you sure?' he asked, secretly building up his hopes.

'Course I am, I wouldn't have asked if I didn't mean it,' came her reply, as she grabbed his hand and started leading him up the stairs.

The first thing he saw, on entering her dimly lit room, was a large crucifix above the bed. Pictures of serpents and other ghoulish creatures decorated the walls, all artistically drawn but still too morbid to look at for long. In the corner stood a large, glass cabinet, in which an enormous snake lay coiled amongst the greenery.

'I knew you liked snakes, but you never mentioned you kept one,' he said, peering into the cabinet.

'Didn't I? Oh, sorry. You don't mind, do you? Usually people run a mile when I mention I keep snakes.'

'No, I don't mind. It's something that makes you special,' he responded, trying to sound complimentary. He looked around the room. 'You said snakes, but I can only see one…how many do you have?'

'Five, the rest are in the other rooms. I'll show you later if you like?'

He nodded, telling her he would love to, before going on to ask how she got into snakes. She seemed pleased.

'I didn't know you'd be so interested. In my last job, I had a supervisor who was into snakes. I saw them when she invited me in one night—' she stopped and changed the subject. 'But I didn't bring you up here to talk about snakes. Shall we get on with it?'

Perhaps she did play for the other team, he thought. Had an affair with her female supervisor? No, more likely bi. He and Evelyn had often kissed, so she must go in for men as well; after all, it was she who had invited him up to her room. I bet none of the others got this far, he thought, before bringing his concentration back to their conversation. 'Of course, sorry. It was just a bit of a surprise, that's all.'

'Most people are surprised,' she said, before pointing to the large double bed. 'Take off your shoes before you lie down.'

Anticipation grew as he followed her instructions. This was it. The others had never got this far. As he took his place on the black satin sheets she went over to the stereo unit, turned on the radio and adjusted the volume. She looked at the clock and smiled.

‘Good, we still have time.’

Still have time? he asked himself, as she joined him on the bed. Time before her partner arrived home? Possibly, though unlikely given what he already knew about her. Housemate or parents, perhaps? The house was large enough, too large for just her, though he was sure she would have mentioned if she were sharing or living with her parents…why would she want to keep that a secret? No, it must be a partner, in which case he needed to move fast. Time was obviously of the essence.

Three minutes to ten and she showed no resistance to his affection. Kissing, soft at first, then passionately; they had rarely been this close before. Her proximity felt good, especially in the privacy of her bedroom. Yet he could not help but notice her eyes, constantly watching the clock. It was off putting, as was the radio which was far too loud for his liking. The ten o’clock news came and went. A music track started playing, during which she grew increasingly agitated, followed by a commercial break. He pulled her in tighter and increased the ferocity of his kissing.

Suddenly, she released her hold of him, rolling onto her back and wriggling away from him. Perhaps he had gone too far? Frustrated and confused, he lay there in silence. Then he felt her hand take hold of his.

'Quick, close your eyes,' she whispered.

He ignored her request and went to kiss her again. She pushed him away.

'No! Take my hand,' she insisted. 'Come on, do as I say.'

He did as she instructed, and they both lay there, side by side, holding hands with their eyes closed.

'What's going on?' he asked, somewhat bemused.

'Shush, concentrate on the radio. Relax and allow your mind to drift but keep concentrating on the radio.'

'What's so special about a commercial break?'

'Just be quiet and do it, okay?' came her harsh response.

Her increasing forcefulness surprised him, and he decided it would be easiest to play along. The commercial ended, and the music resumed. It was an easy listening station, so he would have expected the music to be soothing, but this particular track was totally out of place: a fast-paced TV theme.

'That's the theme to—'

'Be quiet! Relax and let your mind drift,' she said, cutting him short.

Keeping his eyes closed and mind open, he noticed vague images developing in his mind, becoming brighter and more distinct with every moment. 'Wow! This is fantastic,' he exclaimed.

'Yes, but don't let go of my hand. Just stay calm and relaxed. Let your mind take over, it's difficult to begin with but you'll get used to it.'

As the music slowly faded from his head, the images became clearer. He was in a library. An old library, with wooden shelves, stacked high with a mixture of crisp, new, and dusty, old books. The only light came from candles and oil lamps, distributed haphazardly along the walls and on the tables, and a strange, warm, yellow-golden glow. This light emanated from an opening in the floor, out of which the top rungs of an old-fashioned wooden ladder were poking out.

'This is unbelievable,' he gasped, trying to make sense of it all. Evelyn was standing next to him. Her lips remained closed, but he could hear her voice.

'I said I'd take you somewhere fantastic,' the voice said.

He went to speak.

'No, just think of what you want to say; we can communicate telepathically.'

He looked around in amazement. He could not quite comprehend what had just happened. He started questioning her, trying to reign in his curiosity and only ask one question at a time. 'How did you find out about this place? Experimentation? Experience?'

'Actually, I found it by accident. I was listening to the radio one night, you know, dozing off, half asleep. Then this track came on…and my mind bought me here.'

'How many times have you been?'

'I tried it again the next night, and the same thing happened. It seems the station plays the same track at the same time every night, and each time I listen, this happens.'

'Have you told anyone else?'

'Only my friend, Jo, and the same happened for her. We've both been here several times. Individually at first, until she suggested she came to mine. That's how we found out we could come here together if we held hands.'

'Have you come up with any theories?' he asked, still trying to take it all in.

'Jo's more technically minded, and she says there might be a signal buried in the music, something which affects the mind.'

'So other people might be experiencing the same thing?'

'Maybe, but unless they are physically connected to someone else, like we are now, they will be alone in their experiences.'

'I see,' he mused, still awestruck. 'So, there may be others here too?' He wanted to know everything and was about to ask another question before she stopped him.

'We'll talk about it later, okay? Let's explore first.'

'Good idea,' he said. 'Though we won't have much time, the track will be finished in a minute.'

'That's the other thing. While we're in this state, time is compressed, like a dream. A moment can seem to last for hours when only a few seconds have passed. Complicated I know, but the upshot is that we have all the time in the world. The other night, Jo and I spent what felt like an entire day here, but when we returned the record was still playing.'

'Amazing.' He grinned at her. 'When can we start?' She smiled back and walked him over to the bookshelves.

'Pick a book, any book.'

He selected a book at random.

'Take it to the table,' she said, pointing to a large table in the centre of the room.

He placed the book on its polished wooden surface.

'Open it.'

As soon as he opened the book, a miniature ladder appeared right in the middle of the page, surrounded by the same golden glow as the ladder on the floor of the room. 'Wow!' he gasped.

'Yeah. Now, tell me what book it is,' Evelyn asked.

He carefully lifted the book, so as not to disturb the ladder, and read out the title on the spine: 'Treasure Island.'

'Right, now place the book on the floor and take hold of the ladder. See? It's getting bigger. We could climb down if we wanted to; the ladder takes you into the story, so if we went down, we would be able to experience Treasure Island, as if it was real.'

Adam gathered the same would happen with all the books and was about to suggest they look for their favourite titles before she interrupted him.

'So far, Jo and I have only selected a few well-known titles, but it works every time.'

'Great! Have they got The Hobbit? Or better still, Fifty Shades,' he added, raising an eyebrow.

'I would imagine so,' she sniggered, 'Jo asked for that one too, but we haven't found it yet. Anyway, tonight we're just going to use the ladder in the floor. You never know where it's going to lead, could be anywhere. It's completely random, potluck really. We've been to all sorts of places: the Arctic, where we had a snow fight; New York, where—'

'Anywhere?' he interrupted before she could finish. She smiled at the interruption.

'Yep, anywhere.'

He moved towards the ladder. 'What are we waiting for, then? Come on!'

'You first,' she said, holding the top the ladder.

Adam peered into the seemingly bottomless chasm beneath him as he gingerly placed his foot on the fourth rung down. The yellow glow surrounded them like a mist, gradually fading to reveal a bright blue sky as they descended further. Passing through warm sunshine, it took them only a few minutes to cover what felt like hundreds of feet of atmosphere. Soon, he was stepping off the final rung onto a small patch of grass, surrounded by trees. Evelyn followed a few seconds later.

'Here we are then,' she said with a broad smile.

He asked her whether she had been to this place before, but she declined.

'Remember, the ladder takes you to a different place every time'.

'Incredible. Shall we take a look around?' he asked. 'If you're right about time being compressed, we don't need to worry about rushing back.' She beamed at the suggestion, probably glad that he had so far accepted what was happening without much resistance, and pleased he was as keen for adventure as she was.

'Lead the way then,' she said, gesturing towards a dusty path which led into the distance.

Walking through woodland and the occasional clearing, an hour must have passed before they came to a wall, the type you would expect to find surrounding a large country estate. It had obviously been there for some years, and they would have missed it completely had there not been a gap in the surrounding bushes. As they investigated further, moving aside some of the branches that obscured the wall, they found a large, wooden door. There were no clues as to what was on the other side, but that was part of the adventure: a journey into the unknown. There might be a castle, or perhaps a palace; they could not wait to open the door and find out. After several minutes of pushing, kicking, and shoving, the door finally creaked open to reveal what appeared to be a garden. Once well-kept, it was now a neglected wasteland; nature's reclamation had taken its toll and the lawns were jungles of tall grass which almost blocked their view of the flower beds, which were now no more than a mass of weeds and unkempt plants. Eventually, they found a pathway, which led them to a dilapidated greenhouse. Where they still existed, the panes of glass were stained green from years of weathering, but many had been shattered as a result of plants growing wild inside. It looked a sad affair. Even sadder was the main house, which they found further down the path amongst a dense clump of trees.

Evelyn loved the house. Its state of dereliction suited her gothic personality, and the moment they arrived she dragged Adam by the arm to take a look inside. The surrounding trees meant there was hardly any light inside the house, and like the greenhouse, many of the windows had been broken by overgrown branches. Surprisingly, it was still furnished, though years of weathering and neglect meant it was totally uninhabitable. Adam could not help but question what had happened.

'I wonder how such a magnificent house came to be abandoned?'

'Especially with the furniture still in place,' added Evelyn. 'The inhabitants must have been forced to leave in a hurry, leaving the place to become what it is now.'

'Perhaps the previous owner died, with no apparent heir to inherit? Or maybe there was a dispute over the will…whatever the reason—'

Evelyn butted in. 'Whatever the reason, I love it. Come on, let's explore!'

And explore they did, wandering through the vast house; investigating; imagining; playing. They chased one another around the downstairs rooms and envisaged having fantastic banquets at the enormous table which stood in the dining hall, fully laid out ready for a meal to be served. They created an extensive family tree based on the portraits hanging from the walls and pretended to entertain important visitors in the lounge, from long dead prime ministers to royalty to foreign heads of state.

Upstairs, Evelyn was in her gothic element. In the darkness, she created a world of vampires and werewolves, spirits, devils, and goblins. Adam gazed in wonderment as she played out numerous fantasies on one of the giant four-poster beds. She pretended to have been taken by a winged serpent, thrashing about in feigned ecstasy as it ravished her. He was captivated by the way she shrieked and withered with excitement amongst the dusty, old sheets. How he wished he could take the place of the serpent.

He climbed onto the bed and lay down beside her. At first, she was receptive to his light kisses, but she must have sensed his intentions and it was not long before she shuffled across the bed away from him. The atmosphere had changed, and she quickly suggested they try exploring somewhere else. He was disappointed, but what could he do? In a way, this was her world; he had little choice but to surrender to her wishes.

'How do we do that?' he asked, somewhat disheartened.

'Simple. Just think of the ladder and it will reappear.'

'Like this?' he said, thinking of the ladder.

'Exactly. Except this time, we've got to go up,' she replied, climbing off the bed, and walking towards the ladder, which had appeared at the far side of the room.

He was just a few steps behind when she looked back.

'I'll lead this time,' she said, stepping onto the bottom rung. 'Right, here goes.' She started climbing.

This time the ladder took them back to her room. Adam looked around, disappointed. 'Suppose that's it for tonight.'

'No, this is still the dream. Listen. We can't hear the radio. It should still be on, but you can never hear it during the dreams.'

'Oh, right,' he said. 'So how do we get out of the dream then?'

'When you're ready you just think about opening your eyes, but don't do it just yet, I want to see why it's brought us back here.'

'It looks just the same as before—' Adam stopped dead; his eyes fixed on the other side of the room.

Evelyn followed his gaze and looked shocked to see the snake sliding out of its cabinet, along the top of the dresser and down onto the floor. They stood in complete silence as it continued slithering, over the purple carpet and onto the bed, where it stopped and held Evelyn in its stare.

'Do you often let it out of the cabinet,' Adam asked in whisper, too frightened to raise his voice in case the noise startled the snake into attacking.

'Usually Asmodeus is quite playful, but now he doesn't seem happy, does he?' Evelyn replied, in an equally hushed voice.

'You can say that again. What do we do, you're the snake expert?'

'I don't know, he's never been like this, and he's never got himself out of the cabinet before.'

'Perhaps we could stare him out, let him decide what he wants to do next, he might go back?' whispered Adam.

'Good idea. Then, when he starts to move away, I'll grab him and put him back in his cabinet. It's not a good idea to reach for him while he's staring at us.'

At that moment, the snake looked up to the ceiling, where another yellow glow had appeared. Out of the brightest point in the centre came one of the now familiar ladders. The snake's stare followed the ladder as it descended to the bed, and as the ladder drew closer, they noticed the snake's look of fierceness begin to subside. Besides welcoming the intrusion, they could only watch as the snake slid onto the bottom rung.

'Grab him,' said Adam in loud whisper.

'No, not yet. Let's wait to see where he goes. I'm fascinated, this is all new.'

They stared as the snake twisted its long slender body up the ladder, systematically slithering in and out of the rungs as it steadily made its way towards the candescent light emanating from the ceiling. It had almost reached the top when the ladder started lifting.

'Quick, let's follow before the ladder disappears,' Evelyn gasped, hurriedly dragging Adam by the arm.

They only just made it onto the bottom rungs before the ladder disappeared into the yellow chasm. With the ladder ascending, there was little climbing to be done, and soon they passed through the yellow mist into the open air. It was a bright autumn morning, and they watched as the snake left the ladder behind, making its way through the reds and golds of fallen leaves before passing through the bars of an iron gate, outside a churchyard.

The gates, each with a large serpent forged in their centre, had obviously received a recent coating of oil, as they were easy to open despite being old and rusty. Following the snake, they wandered through the churchyard and passed through a pair of large oak doors, which led them into a small country chapel. The chapel was in semi-darkness, the only light coming from the multicoloured streams of daylight pouring through the stained-glass windows. It was clearly harvest time, as the altar was decorated with generous offerings of fruit, vegetables, and decorative bread loaves. Behind the altar was a small apple tree, which the snake had started to climb.

Though they subconsciously accepted that they were still in a dream, the solitary beam of light currently illuminating the tree and the snake made the whole scene feel eerie and surreal. Nothing appeared to have come about by chance; it was as if the snake knew exactly where to go and what to do. It had expected to see and start ascending the ladder in the bedroom, slither through the gates and into the chapel, and find the apple tree, which it was now climbing without hesitation.

Evelyn stood frozen as she watched the spectacle, her eyes transfixed on the snake as it took a solitary apple from one the branches and slid down the tree. She continued staring as she stepped forward, freezing again when she reached the snake, which still held the freshly picked apple in its mouth. Raising the fruit to within inches of her face, the animal was enticing her to take it. Evelyn slowly leant forward until her lips touched the apple. As she took a bite, both she and the snake were engulfed in the same golden light that had surrounded the ladders. She appeared to be in a trance, taking the apple from the snake and biting into it for a second time. A third time. Each bite bigger than the last. The snake slid towards her, and she offered no resistance, allowing it to crawl over her. She seemed willing as it eased her to the floor, entwining itself around her body so they appeared to be one entity.

Adam could only stare, paralysed with indecision. Should he fight the snake off her? Should he simply wait to see how the situation unfolded? The snake looked larger than it had been in the bedroom, too powerful for him to handle by himself, and Evelyn was in no state to assist. He had best be cautious. All he could do was watch and hope.

Hypnotised into submission, Evelyn lay on her back on the steps leading up to the altar, gazing at the roof while the snake continued to wrap its extensive body around her. She managed to free her arms and stretch them along the top step, gulping as the serpent tightened its grip, then sighing with relief as the pressure was released.

Adam still felt helpless, yet continued to stare, mesmerised by Evelyn's look of joy as the snake started sliding under her t-shirt. Dangerous as the situation was, he was intrigued by the spectacle, imagining what the snake must be feeling as it surveyed the smoothness of Evelyn's naked flesh. Somehow, it managed to undo her jeans, and Evelyn arched her back and gasped in ecstasy as the serpent explored further.

She still held the apple and was holding it out to him, beckoning Adam to take a bite. Temptation. But he knew he had to resist, afraid that acceptance meant he too would fall under the spell of the snake. Evelyn caressed the fruit, waving it seductively. It looked enticing…what harm would one bite do? If he kept his distance, he would be fine. Cautiously, he stepped forward, leant over towards Evelyn's outstretched hand, and took a bite into the apple's red flesh. Immediately, a feeling of warmth and happiness came over him. Evelyn nodded in approval. This must be what she felt, a sensation of love, and abandonment. She lured him into taking another bite. This time the feeling was stronger. Now he understood how she had succumbed to the snake: the feeling of rapture was too much; she could not have cared about anything other than this feeling.

From beneath Evelyn's clothing, the snake raised its head to look at Adam, causing her shirt to lift. For the first time, Adam caught a glimpse of her exposed torso. Alternating his gaze between Evelyn's pure freshness and the snake, he was sure he saw what appeared to be a faint smirk on the snake's face. The snake held Adam in its gaze, teasing him, as its long body continued to slide over Evelyn. It was playing on his desire, knowing that Adam had just witnessed her rawness and now more than ever wanted her intimacy.

Evelyn was still holding out the apple, and Adam quickly snatched it away so he could take a deeper bite. He offered it back, and she provocatively took several more bites, juice oozing down her chin. She thrust the apple towards him, and as he finished it his desire for her became overwhelming. Snake or no snake, he wanted her, and he wanted her now. He heard her voice in his head.

'Make love to me. Take me, have me, take me, here, now,' it moaned.

He heard another voice too. A soft rhythmic voice. It could only have been that of the snake.

'Take her, take Eve, now. Show her your desire. You have both tasted the fruit, now let her taste your love.'

He was dumbstruck. He knew exactly what he should do...knew what he wanted to do...but should he? Was this right? In a chapel, now? He hesitated, before he heard the voice again, as if the snake had read his thoughts.

'Go on, Adam, take Eve. Take Eve. Take her. Now.'

II

Evelyn did not come in to work the next day. Adam vaguely remembered her saying she had been planning to visit friends, but he could not help thinking of the night before and wondering whether that was the real reason for her absence. It might just have been a fantasy, created by some outside source via the radio, but it had all seemed so real. How he wished it could have continued, but just as he had been about to make love to her, Evelyn had let go of his hand and opened her eyes, breaking their contact. The snake, the altar, and the chapel had all disappeared, leaving himself and Evelyn lying on the bed, where they had been the whole time.

Evelyn's expression had been guarded, almost certainly because of what had happened on the altar steps, and after a long silence he had been the one to gingerly start up a conversation. They had spent a long time discussing the dream, in the end both agreeing that they had not been themselves and had not been in control of their own actions. Evelyn had suggested they give the radio a rest for a while, regroup, and then try it again sometime later.

Her request did not stop Adam, though. The events of the previous night had given him a taste for adventure, and he was determined to try it for himself, Evelyn, or no Evelyn. Back at home, in the privacy of his own bedroom, he switched on the radio and closed his eyes. At first, there was nothing. Remembering what Evelyn had said about letting his mind relax, he cleared his thoughts, allowing nothing to creep in, not even thoughts of ladders and fantastic journeys. Suddenly, a minute into the music track, he was back in the library. He looked for others, perhaps Evelyn, who he suspected would also be unable to resist trying again. But then he remembered: people only saw each other if they were holding hands or making some other form of physical contact. Even if Evelyn were there, she would be unaware that he had broken his side of the agreement.

It took a while to adjust to the experience. He did not have Evelyn as a guide this time, but he felt sure he could manage; if he experienced any problems all he had to do was open his eyes. Just as before, there was a yellow glow in the centre of the room, with the top of a ladder poking out. Looking around at the shelves, he thought of taking a book and checking it out but decided against it. Perhaps next time. For now, he really wanted to see where the main ladder would take him. He wanted to explore the unknown, like they had done the night before; as Evelyn had done on numerous occasions, either alone or with her friend Jo.

Adam had been correct about Evelyn's inability to resist another journey. Alone in her room, she too had turned on the radio and was waiting for the music to start. More accustomed to the experience than Adam, she lost no time in making for the main ladder, and after a short descent came to a large cellar, which she assumed must be beneath a mansion or some other sizeable building. At one end sat a silver metallic cube, and it was evident that someone had either been monitoring it or conducting experiments: attached were an assortment of different coloured wires and cables, connected to a collection of monitors and sensors. Contemplating the story behind the cube, even what form of experimentation might be taking place, Evelyn hesitantly walked over for a closer inspection. The cube looked too large to have been carried down the stairs, or even pushed through the coal chute, and stroking its smooth surface she felt the coolness of solid steel. She tapped it, but there was no sound. She tapped it again, this time harder. Even after a hefty thump of her fist she failed to hear a sound. Seeing a hammer on a nearby workbench, she struck the cube. This time she heard a muffled clang, but no echo, so either the cube had a thick casing or was completely solid. She wondered what could possibly be inside, perhaps that was the reason for the experimentation? She touched it again, jumping away in surprise on receiving a nasty static shock.

Looking around the cellar, all she could see, aside from the cube and electrical equipment, was a work bench and some old pieces of furniture. The only light came from the monitors, and a solitary low wattage bulb in the centre of the ceiling, which was reflected by the shiny surface of the cube. Evelyn wondered how the cube had come to be there in the first place. Had it been there before the house was built, perhaps? She thought about the rest of the house. Maybe she would find the answers to her questions if she explored a little further.

In the corner of the cellar was an old wooden staircase, which led to a trapdoor in the ceiling. Evelyn climbed up to it, but to her dismay she found that the door was locked. Never mind, there was still the coal chute, she thought, climbing back down, and making her way across the room. But when she reached the chute, she found it too was locked. Evelyn sighed, frustrated that her plans to investigate had been ruined. There was no obvious way out. She would just have to think of the ladder and explore somewhere else.

Lowering himself down the ladder, Adam found himself on a dirt track in the middle of a wood. It was summer-time and sweat was already running down his back as he perused where the ladder had taken him. Taking off his sweatshirt and tying it around his waist, in an effort to stay cool, he looked back and forth, trying to determine which way to go. The path looked the same in both directions, so he took a chance and opted to travel the way he was facing. It turned out to be a good move; after fifteen minutes of walking he arrived at an old, abandoned double-decker bus, sitting atop an even older concrete plinth. Adam assumed that the concrete plinth had once held a shed, which he guessed might have been used by the Forestry Commission, or some other organisation, to store equipment. The bus looked as though it had been there for some time; its once bright, red paintwork was now a faded pink, and its windows and doors had been stained green by the surrounding foliage.

He took a few moments to consider how the bus had come to be deposited in the middle of a wood. Had it been brought here by a local preservation group, who could not afford the upkeep, perhaps? Or by a group of ex-drivers, who fell out over who should take charge of looking after it? Whatever the reason, he wondered what it was used for these days. During warm summer evenings and school holidays, he imagined that gangs from the surrounding area must have an unwritten truce as to who utilised it as their den, and when. Then, during the cold winter months, it probably acted as a night shelter for the area's homeless.

Contemplating was not enough for Adam; he was eager to see for himself, and after quickly checking that no one else was around, he made his way inside. Hot, musty air hit him as he pushed open the door of the central entrance. Unsurprisingly, the interior of the bus was just as ramshackle as its exterior. Most of the faded blue seats were covered in a concoction of unmentionable stains, and the walls and windows were a mass of graffiti: a mixture of local gang tag names and favourite football teams.

Upstairs, the situation was much the same, except that the graffiti now included the names of various couples, who had apparently used the bus to enjoy a private moment together. Adam could see why this place had appealed to these young lovers: high in the air, and partially hidden by the surrounding foliage, the upper deck was the ideal spot for intimacy. Indeed, amongst the discarded fast food wrappings, newspapers, porn magazines, and other assorted rubbish, he found several used condoms, as well as two pairs of women's underwear, one pair of men's boxer shorts, a bra and a black stiletto.

Finding himself a fairly clean seat, he decided to take a moment to rest. The bus was similar, if not identical, to the ones he used every day on the number twenty-four route, which took him from Hampstead to Whitehall, where he worked with Evelyn. Allowing his mind to drift, he recreated some of the scenes he had witnessed on those daily commutes: a smartly dressed gentleman, with expensive jewellery and a Burberry scarf, talking into his mobile phone, his hand covering his mouth to prevent any lip-reading industrial spies from catching his conversation; an attractive girl shouting for her distant friends to wait, while she struggled to master the 'Boris' bikes they were riding; the mobile ticket inspector trying to explain to an elderly tourist that she had to buy a ticket from the roadside ticket machine before riding the bus. The bus was always a good place from which to watch the drama of daily life unfold. A few days previously, he had seen a young couple arguing in an alleyway next to a pub. Obviously the worse for drink, the man had been shielding himself from the woman's blows as they argued. Perhaps more intriguing had been the heavily pregnant teenage girl looking anxiously on.

The sound of voices snapped him out of his daydream. Jumping up with a start, he hoped whoever it was would avoid coming upstairs. Like him, they probably thought the bus was empty, and would be surprised to find someone waiting for them. He stayed still. They were female voices, girls most likely, probably making the most of the long summer break. He wanted to leave. The heat on the top deck was too intense; he had to move. But all he could do was stand there, immobilised in horror as the voices grew louder. They were coming up the stairs. He wracked his brains, trying to think of something to say when they saw him.

His relief was immeasurable when one of the girls decided they were better off staying downstairs.

'It's always too bleeding hot up there in the summer,' she said, dragging her friend back down the stairs.

At least he was safe from being seen, though he now had no way of escaping the heat. He considered creeping down the stairs, but from the proximity of their voices, he could tell they had chosen the seats right next to the staircase. He had no desire to intrude on their private conversation, and they would almost certainly suspect him to be stalker, or worse, if they found him there. Hopefully, they would not stay for too long. For now, he had no choice but to stay where he was.

Evelyn thought of the ladder, expecting it to appear in front of her. Nothing happened. She closed her eyes and thought again, expecting to see a welcoming yellow glow when she opened them. Again, there was nothing. She stood beneath the coal chute, thinking of what else she could do, when the printer on the work bench suddenly came to life. She walked over to look, but she could not decipher any of the data being printed. A few seconds later, the nearby seismograph started twitching. She glanced at the monitors and gasped, as long banks of figures started to whirl up and down the screens. Whatever these instruments were measuring, it was happening. Now.

She looked towards the cube. Not only was it vibrating, but it had also started to glow and was emitting a muted whistling sound. The vibration strengthened and the whistling became a screech, then a high-pitched screaming sound. Scanning the cellar, Evelyn's eyes focused on a pair of industrial ear protectors, resting on the top of an old toolbox. Whoever was conducting the experiments here obviously expected there to be a lot of noise. Either that, or they wore ear projectors as a matter of routine. Regardless, as soon as she put them on, the sound became bearable. But only for a short while. Soon they were providing little protection, as the noise became intolerable again. The high-pitched squeal started making everything in the cellar vibrate, and she feared her head might split in two. Her sight was already beginning to blur. She tried to look at the screens, and despite their violent shaking she could still see the speed at which the data was being registered. The radiance from the cube was now so bright that she had to use to her hands to shield her eyes.

The sound of a cigarette being offered, and the striking of matches, told him the girls were going to be there for longer than he had anticipated. The heat was really starting to get to him and sweat was pouring down his face. He needed to make a move; he would just have to be brave and face the consequences. He started to tread carefully towards the staircase when an alternative exit strategy came to mind. The ladder. If he thought of the ladder, it should appear in front of him, giving him a safe and easy route away from this stifling heat and uncomfortable situation. He could explore somewhere else, somewhere cooler.

Almost as soon as the thought of the ladder it appeared before him, right next to the front seats. He lost no time, climbing onto the top rungs and lowering himself down as quickly as he could. Though he knew it was not her, one of the girls sounded just like Evelyn, and as he descended the ladder, he could not help but think of her, and her friend Jo. He wondered if Jo, too, was a goth. In many ways, he was envious of this Jo. She and Evelyn seemed to have had numerous adventures together: snowball fights; city sightseeing…it all sounded fun and interesting. He wished he could have joined them. More than that, he was worried that they shared more than just friendship. Could his colleague have been right about Evelyn? Was she a closet lesbian? In which case, were she and Jo lovers?

Downheartedness and jealousy were taking over his thoughts, so much so that he missed his footing and fell the final few feet. The moist softness of a patch of grass broke his fall, but the impact knocked him senseless. Next thing he knew, he was sitting up, recovering from the shock of falling. As his eyes adjusted, it dawned on him that it was early evening, and he was in the town where he had grown up. Evelyn had told him there was no order to where the ladder took you, it was entirely random. But for it to bring him here…it was uncanny. Had whatever caused these strange dreams been watching him? Had it detected his fall and his subsequent anxiety, deciding to bring him to a place where he had once felt safe and secure?

Either the noise was abating, or she was getting used to it, for she could only hear a quiet hum now. She had heard something like it before: the low-pitched mantra of a multitude of voices, the chanting of Buddhist monks or some other religious sect. The mellow, hypnotic sound resonated in her head, creating a feeling of euphoria. Perhaps it was her mind lulling her into a sense of security, trying to drown out her fears of what might come next? It was not working. Fear was still at the back of her mind; not knowing was her greatest terror.

She tried closing then opening her eyes, to escape this nightmare and return to the safety of her bed. But like before, when she had wished for the ladder to appear, nothing happened. This dream was as real as reality, and she was trapped. Panic joined the fear. Next thing she knew, she was levitating. At first, suspended in the air, then being pulled towards the cube. As she floated closer, the heat from the glare grew stronger. Surely, she would be burnt to a cinder if she went any closer? But she was still being pulled. By now, the feeling of euphoria had been overtaken by panic. She felt the extreme heat against her skin. Smoke started to rise from her clothing. She closed her eyes, preparing for the inevitable doom.

What if his own brain was now controlling the dream, creating somewhere he felt secure in response to his fear? A sort of 'safety valve', perhaps? Could be. Unfortunately, Adam had no way of finding out, not there and then anyway. He might as well explore whilst he was here. After all, that had kind of been the point of entering this dream state in the first place.

His hope that the next place would be cooler had been fulfilled. It had clearly been raining just before he had arrived, the reflection of the streetlamps in the damp road breaking the twilight. On the other side of the road, people were making their way along the pavement, and he could not help noticing the vacant expressions on their faces. Was it the dullness of the wet evening? Or because it was midwinter? The latter was more likely. There were no leaves on the trees, and there was a sharp chill in the air. Christmas must have already come and gone, and now there was nothing to look forward to but the cold winter months, before the warmth of the spring broke the spell of melancholy. If only these people would take a moment to stop and look at the beauty around them. The glow from the shop windows glistening in the damp roadway, made more beautiful by the rising moon, shining between the breaks in the clouds. The sight was sufficient to lift any downtrodden spirits, well, his anyway.

Evelyn was lying in an ocean of yellow nothingness. She could feel a floor beneath her, but could not see it, and smoke continued to rise from her clothing as she sat up. New surroundings. But wherever she was, she was safe. She was alive. Or was she? Wasn't this what death was all about, the emptiness of no longer existing?

Winding his way along the unchanged street, Adam was reminded of his mother. The haberdashery shop where his mother had worked was still there, as was the butcher's, grocer's, and post office. He was tempted to wait outside the haberdashers for his mother, expecting her to walk out at any moment. But his common sense reminded him that those days were long gone. These days, thoughts of his mother only brought sadness, and his expression of melancholy now matched the faces of the people around him.

Alone, he walked up the steady incline, matching the pace of the commuters who were making their way home for the night. He walked past the inn, busy with market traders who were just taking down their stalls for the day, past the walled hill, upon which stood the parish church, towards the medieval castle.

A powerful, male voice made Evelyn jump.

'What are you doing here?' boomed the voice, amidst the nothingness.

Her state of bewilderment meant it took her a while to realise that the voice was addressing her.

'What are you doing here?' it repeated, this time with more determination.

'I was beginning to wonder that myself,' Evelyn replied cautiously, trying to identify who the owner of the voice was.

'How did you get here?' asked the voice, sounding frustrated that she was not providing the answer it was seeking.

'I don't know! One minute I was—' she paused, trying to remember. 'I can't remember…I climbed down the ladder, but my memory is completely blank after that.' She was still trying to figure out who was talking to her. 'Where are you?' she asked. 'I can hear you, but I can't see you.'

'Of course, you can see me,' said the voice. 'Try looking a little harder.'

Again, she glanced around at the nothingness, but there was no one to be seen. Whoever was talking to her, they were obviously playing games. 'I still can't see you. Stop messing around or I'll—'

'Or you will what?' asked the voice.

It had started to rain again, as Adam followed the track leading up to the castle, and the rain fell increasingly heavily as the track steepened. He continued trudging up the hill as the roughness of the ancient walls became more pronounced. He drew closer…closer…making his way over the slippery wooden drawbridge, which was always open to allow for visitors, stumbling through a massive, stone archway, and finally stepping into the castle. He stared in awe at the enormity of the place. Despite having visited the castle thousands of times before, he had never been able to get over the sheer size of this incredible building.

Realising that the owner of the voice could see her, but she could not see them, Evelyn knew they had the upper hand. 'Simple. I won't speak to you,' she replied, in response to the voice's previous query. 'I'll ignore you completely. You'll soon get fed up talking to yourself, and then you'll go away.'

The voice laughed humourlessly. 'And then what? You will stay here forever, amongst this barren nothingness? Yes, I will eventually get bored, but not as bored you will become. Yes, I will ultimately go away, but can you? Where would you go? At least I have the option of returning to where I came from. The same cannot be said for you.'

Evelyn was suddenly afraid. Much that she hated to admit it, the voice was right. If she wanted to get out of this place, she needed to cooperate. 'Okay, fine, I'll talk. But at least make yourself visible. I refuse to talk to a disembodied voice. And you have to tell me who you are—' She stopped. The now familiar yellow glow was forming in front of her. Her heart lifted. A ladder! She could escape! But much to her dismay, there was no ladder. Instead, she saw the figure a man, standing in front of a wooden door.

Adam had already acquired an excellent knowledge of the castle. He had spent much of his childhood playing there; it was important enough for historians to have written books about it, and to have been the subject of a television documentary. The castle's fame meant it was also well-maintained, and like most preserved castles it still had its fair share of state rooms, feasting halls, royal bedrooms, and such like. Everything one would expect from an ancient castle…except…except that, today, it seemed different.

Evelyn could feel his commanding presence, as the male figure approached. He looked younger than his voice had suggested, dressed in a long, white robe, which was unfastened to reveal a smooth muscular chest. She could not help staring at his sculptured torso, and effeminate face. Ordinarily, she would not have given him a second look, but her senses told her that he was special. His voice interrupted her musings.

'You do know you are dead?' he said, in an unassuming way.

'Am I?' she replied, with a distinct lack of surprise. Suddenly, it was all coming back to her: the cellar, the cube…Again, his voice interrupted her thoughts.

'Yes, you are quite dead. You are currently outside what most people call the pearly gates.'

'They don't look very pearly to me, more like an old wooden door. In fact, the same door as my bedroom. I could still be lying on my bed right now, with the radio playing in the background...are you sure that this isn't just another part of the dream?'

'Quite sure. This is Paradise, the afterlife, the next stage—' he paused, adopting a quizzical look. 'What is this nonsense about a dream, and a radio playing?'

'Umm, it's a very long story. I guess you don't know anything about the radio and the dreams then?'

'Obviously not,' the man replied, curtly. He held up an old clipboard, which had appeared out of nowhere, and began to read through a series of names on his list. 'According to my sheet, you—' he stopped. 'Oh, there is nothing listed. You are dead, of course, there can be no arguing with that. Why else would you be here?' He turned the sheet over and began scrutinising another list. 'It is Evelyn, correct?'

Evelyn nodded, as the man continued looking through the list. 'How did you know my name?' she asked. 'I didn't tell you.'

'Oh, we know everything up here,' he replied, without lifting his eyes from the list. 'Hmm, how curious. There is nothing here...' he lowered his clipboard, examining the dark gothic appearance in front of him. 'Ah, I know just where to look,' he declared, turning over several sheets before finding what he was looking for. 'You have been put down for the other place. You like devils, demons, and such like, yes? That means you should not be here.'

Evelyn's face drained as he continued.

'Indeed, according the notes, some of our residents are already protesting against you being here.'

Adam entered the castle through the main archway. Usually, he would have gone straight through to the manicured lawns or main central keep. But this time, the castle was different; he was presented with the additional option of turning left or right, along a series of narrow walkways which he presumed ran between the inner and outer walls. He remembered the keep, but not the walkways. These were new. But, then again, this was a dream. Everything in front of him was a figment of his imagination, and he could only assume that this version of the castle was a variation on his memory of the place. He felt a compulsion to turn left, and after a series of sharp bends, he found himself at the bottom of a spiral staircase. It seemed to go on forever, but eventually he reached the top, and was greeted by a series of rooms.

He had always been fascinated by this place, ever since he was a child, and thought he knew everything there was to know about the castle. But just like the walkways, these rooms were new to him. As a lad, he and his mates had played for hours amongst the towers and battlements, pretending to be knights of the realm; fighting battles and running off with their spoils, usually some princess they had supposedly rescued. Over the years he had developed a more serious interest in this place; at university he had written his dissertation on the castle's history, and had later suggested to the local paranormal group that they investigate the ghosts which were said to haunt the place. Sadly, the request had been denied by English Heritage, but it had been worth a shot.

Evelyn took a step back. 'Who is complaining?' she asked. 'There's no harm in being gothic, it's quite acceptable these days. And we don't all worship devils and demons you know.'

'Be that as it may, there have been protests regarding your presence here.'

'Who are you, anyway?' Evelyn asked defiantly, putting her hands on her hips. 'You look too young to be Saint Peter.'

'You are both mistaken, and correct. I am Saint Peter.'

'Really? You look far too young, you should be an old man, with a white beard and all that.'

'I did once look like that, two-thousand years ago or so. But I have changed my appearance since then. I now look as I did—'

'Wait a second. You're saying that you died old, then turned young again?' interrupted Evelyn, cutting him short. 'And that you won't, or can't, let me in?'

'Correct, on both accounts,' replied the young Saint Peter.

'Right...why can't you let me in exactly? Besides being a goth, I haven't done anything bad, not really. Others have done worse, far worse.'

Saint Peter looked her up and down in disgust. 'It says gothic devil worshiper on my list. That is more than enough to refuse entry and send you to the other place.'

Evelyn was panicking now. 'Hold on, that's not strictly true. I've been to church a few times, and I know loads of really religious people...'

Wandering through the mysterious rooms, Adam was sure that he should be standing on top of the castle battlements by now. It was so strange, everything looked completely different, like he was somewhere else entirely. Or perhaps he was still in the castle, but just at a different time. Yes, that could explain it. During his research, he had discovered that a large manor house once stood on the site of the castle, owned by a local lord who had pleased the then king by having it demolished, to make way for a castle. The more he thought about it, the more certain he became that he was currently inside the manor house.

Apparently, there were ghosts in the manor too, for as he wandered amongst the richly furnished rooms, fifteenth century he decided, he could hear voices. Not those of other visitors, whispering reverently about this historic place, but those of people going about their daily business. He listened to heated arguments; friends and close acquaintances having jovial conversations; the sound of children playing, whispering secrets they wanted to keep hidden from their elders. Were these the voices previous visitors had heard…the voices they had interpreted as ghosts? It was possible. He certainly hoped that, if this were the case, these past inhabitants were simply going about their daily lives in their own real time and would not notice his presence.

Saint Peter's eyes narrowed. 'Everyone goes to church: christenings, weddings, funerals, Christmas services. Perfunctory attendance is not sufficient for one to be considered religious. Though, if what you say about deeply religious friends is true, that may work in your favour. I will have to go and check. Stay where you are, I will return shortly.'

'Well, I can't exactly go far, what with there being nothing around me but nothingness. I suppose this is what they call purgatory?'

'You are, once again, correct. A perfect description of your current situation. Do not go away.'

'Go where? There's nowhere else to go.'

'Unless you wish to go to the other place, of course. That would save me a lot of trouble.'

'Can you please just get on with it?' sighed Evelyn, before watching the figure of Saint Peter disappear into the yellow mist drifting from the door.

The thought of ghosts unsettled Adam, as he continued to wander through the rooms of the manor house. Dining rooms, drawing rooms, bedrooms…no matter where he went, he continued to hear the voices. Sometimes they were just jumbled sounds; other times, the voices were layered, as though they were all talking over one another. This continued until he arrived at another stone spiral staircase. Suddenly, the voices stopped. Five minutes and many steps later, he was back in the castle.

Walking along a stone passage, he eventually came to a sparsely furnished room. This was more modern than any of the others he had visited, though it was in a severe state of neglect. There was just one armchair, sitting in front of a horribly stained window. The armchair faced outwards, and from the rising haze it was apparent that someone sat there, smoking. As he stepped alongside the chair, his eyes were met by those of an old man, who stared unabashedly back up at him.

The mist reappeared, and from it stepped Saint Peter.

'I have checked with the powers-that-be, and it seems you have a friend in high places. They have recommended that you come in—'

'You mean, I don't have to go to other place?' Evelyn butted in. 'Who is this friend, then?

'I have looked through your full record, and it seems you have not been all bad.'

'See, told you so! Who is this friend in high places, then? I'm intrigued!'

'Miss Magdalene.'

'Who?'

The old man exhaled a puff of smoke and coughed. 'You took your time.'

'I've only just arrived,' retorted Adam, taken back by the old man's brazenness.

'No, you haven't.'

'I have! As soon as I got to the castle, I came up the spiral staircase, through the rooms, then up another staircase, until I reached this room here.'

'Well, you took your time,' said the old man.

'Time?' questioned Adam. 'I've only been here a few hours!'

'A long while then,' replied the old man.

'You were expecting me, I take it?'

'Sort of.' Then, after another long drag on his cigarette, 'What's this about a castle? I can't see a castle.'

'The castle we're in.'

'What castle?'

'This castle—'

'This isn't a castle,' the old man laughed.

'It is!' retorted Adam.

'Is not,' said the man.

'It was when I arrived.'

'Well, it isn't now. Perhaps you need your eyes tested?'

'I am one hundred percent certain that this is a castle.'

'And I'm two hundred percent certain that it's not. Look out of that window and tell me if you see a castle?'

Adam went to the window, and after finding the cleanest patch he peered outside.

'Well, what do you see? Thick, strong walls and towers and battlements?'

There were no walls; no battlements; no central keep…none of the features Adam had expected. 'I see gardens,' he said quietly.

Saint Peter gave a deep sigh. 'Miss Magdalene, one of Master Jesus' closest followers, his wife some might say.'

'Yes, I know who she was, and about the whole wife conspiracy.'

'As I said, some might consider her his wife. I do not. But you will be able to discuss this when you meet her.'

The old man took a long drag on his cigarette. 'And what else?'

'Just gardens. Oh, hang on, there are some sheds at the bottom, and statues, and water fountains in the middle of the flower beds.'

'No castle, then?'

'No, no castle.' Adam looked back at the old man. 'So, where am I?'

'It's not so much a question of where, more a question of when are we.'

'Okay, so, when am I?'

'Oh, come on, shouldn't it be we?'

'All right, when are we?'

Saint Peter sighed, before looking towards the wooden door behind him. 'Fortunately for you, she is here now. Welcome to Heaven, Evelyn. And good luck. You will need it.'

The old man sank into his chair and took one final puff on his cigarette, before throwing the remains to the floor. 'Perhaps you were right to begin with, where are we?'

'You're confusing me now,' said Adam.

'Am I? Oh, sorry. You know, you're actually confusing yourself.'

'I don't think so,' replied Adam, staring at the old man's worn face. 'I knew exactly what was going on before you opened your mouth.'

The old man's nicotine-stained fingers reached beside the cushion and pulled out an old packet of cigarettes. 'Exactly, you are confusing yourself, like I said,' he continued, lifting out another cigarette.

'What do you mean, good luck?' asked Evelyn indignantly. 'This is Paradise, the kingdom of love and happiness and all that.'

'Yes, it is. But you have not yet met Miss Magdalene,' replied Saint Peter, as he turned towards the old wooden door. 'As I said, good luck.'

Adam looked at the floor beside the chair. It was a mess of ash and cigarette ends. As he glanced at the window, he realised the stains resulted from constant exposure to cigarette smoke, and on closer inspection, he noticed that the walls and ceiling were also stained. It was difficult to tell what their original colour had been; the only clues were the faint traces of blue paint in the far corner, the furthest point from where the old man was sitting. The carpet had once been a similar colour, as far as he could tell, though that was also difficult to determine, given the years-worth of ground-in dirt. 'How long have you been here?' Adam asked.

Evelyn's eyes sharpened, as she saw a female figure forming in the mist. As the figure came into focus, Evelyn stared in shock. The woman was a mirror image of herself: her skin was the same colour; she wore the same black jeans and t-shirt…the only difference was that the woman's top had the words 'JC Rules' emblazoned across the chest.

'So, I guess you must be the famous Miss Mary Magdalene?' Evelyn asked, still coming to terms with the fact that she was standing opposite an almost exact replica of herself.

'The one and only,' replied Mary Magdalene, smiling at the surprised expression on Evelyn's face.

'And you're the one who recommended that I should come here?'

'Indeed, I am.'

'But why? According to Saint Peter, I should be in the other place. Which to be honest, I am a little confused about. I don't think I've done anything bad enough to warrant going to Hell...but you've obviously seen my record, so...'

'I have, and that's why I decided you should be here, not there.'

'How long have I been here?' the old man enquired. 'Or should that be, how long have we been here? Or indeed, how long have you been here?'

'You're definitely confusing me now,' stated Adam, trying not to show his frustration at the old man's riddles.

'I think you'll find you're confusing yourself.'

'I am not, I assure you.'

'How do you know?'

'You're talking in riddles.'

'No, you're talking in riddles.'

'I'm talking in riddles?'

'Yes, you are. Can't you tell who I am?' asked the old man incredulously.

'You're an old man, sat in an old chair, in an old room, which has been stained brown because of your years of chain smoking.'

'True...but take a closer look.'

Evelyn stared at Mary Magdalene. 'What do you mean?'

'I need you here.' Mary Magdalene shrugged.

'You need me? But you've already got the great man himself!'

'Oh, JC...he's okay. But he keeps going on and on about love and peace and turning the other cheek...it's getting rather boring to be honest.'

'So, he's boring then?'

'Well...not exactly...he's just...I'm too much of a lady to describe him, really. With all those miracles, you would think...well, put it this way: it would be a miracle if he actually paid me some attention occasionally.'

'He's been neglecting you, then?'

'Let's just say that I've had a lot more fun with those destined for the other place.'

'Weren't you were supposed to be his wife?'

‘Nah, that’s just what later scholars decided. We’re just good friends, with benefits, if you know what I mean? But I need to have something to keep me occupied, while he’s off preaching to the masses and all that.’

‘Wow,’ exclaimed Evelyn. She had never imagined Heaven would be like this. ‘I read once that you were a prostitute, is that a myth too?’

‘It is indeed, but I cannot complain. Considering my somewhat wayward ways, I am not overly surprised.’

‘Didn’t he…didn’t Jesus suspect anything? What would he have done if he had found out?’

‘Remember, Evelyn, he is the one who always goes on about turning the other cheek and sharing one’s worldly possessions. If you think about it, this is just a way for him to share me with others. But let’s put all that aside for the moment. I was going to tell you why I need you.’

‘Ah, yes. Don’t tell me, you’re toying with the idea of becoming a goth—’

Adam examined the old man’s clothing. Despite the material having faded over the years, he could tell that the man was wearing a plain black sweatshirt and black combat trousers, the exact same clothes Adam was wearing himself. Turning his attention to the old man's face, he noticed a small scar just above the man's left eye, and a mole next to his right nostril. The same features that Adam saw in the mirror every morning.

'But...that's impossible! You're me!' Adam exclaimed.

Mary Magdalene's quick response cut Evelyn short. 'Play your cards right and you'll come out of this quite well. Don't forget, anyone can be chosen, and there are some equally interesting people up here.'

'So, I'm here because—'

'You are my ticket to the other place. You're still on their list, so they'll let you in.'

'You want me to take you down there? Won't they recognise you? It would be real coup if they did, you might end up as a hostage or something.'

'No need to worry about that. I have already changed my appearance, though I have to say, I am rather enjoying this new look.'

Mary Magdalene winked, and Evelyn smiled in response. That would explain the outfit then.

'It will only be occasionally, when I want to have a bit of fun,' Mary Magdalene continued. 'You will be free to do as you wish the rest of the time.'

'It sounds a bit dodgy to me...but I do love your outfit.'

'Sexy, isn't it?'

'If you say so...although, dressed identically like this, we do look like a couple of dykes,' laughed Evelyn. 'Seriously though, surely Hell is the last place anyone would want to visit?'

'Not necessarily. You don't know the full story, do you?'

'I know what Hell's like, I'm not stupid.'

'But you only know what the church have taught you.'

'Go on then, enlighten me.'

'It's better than you think.'

'In what way? Hell is perpetual punishment!'

'So they say, but that's only half of the story. Down there, people are perpetually doomed to practice their vices.'

'Go on...'

'Say you were a gambler? You would be doomed to an eternity of gambling. Or if you were a sex addict, an eternity of—'

The old man's face screwed into a laugh. 'Give the man a coconut.'

'But...but...but—' Adam was lost for words.

'But, but, but,' came the old man's sarcastic reply.

'But…how long have you been here?' asked Adam, trying to think rationally.

'Long enough.'

'How long's that?'

'Well, look around! You can see how long, can't you?' laughed the old man.

'A long time,' Adam answered quietly.

The old man laughed again. 'My, my, you're going to have a fine collection of coconuts by the end of this!'

Mary Magdalene stopped mid-sentence, straightening her back. 'Well, anyway, I've been watching you, Evelyn, and I've been extremely impressed.'

'I can see that by the way you're dressed,' laughed Evelyn. 'You don't fancy me, do you?'

'Hmm…I could,' smirked Mary Magdalene. 'I do—'

'But why?' interrupted Evelyn before Mary Magdalene could go any further. 'I'm no one special.'

'Oh, but you are, Evelyn. You're not afraid of exploring, of trying new things. Many up here would have curled up in a ball and cried if they had been confronted with what you have been through.'

'How do you know that?'

'Let's just say I've been watching you from on high. Adam too, cute, isn't he?'

'You been watching Adam as well?'

'You two make a good team. I'm surprised you didn't get together properly you know. I would have.'

'We did, sort of,' replied Evelyn. 'But tell me,' she tried to shift the subject away from Adam. 'Who taught you how to watch over people? Can everyone up here do it?'

'No, no, of course not. Only a few—'

'Like you,' interjected Evelyn. 'But who decides who gets that power?'

'That would be the big man himself.'

'Oh, you mean, God? What's he like? Is he—'

Mary Magdalene laughed.

'What's so funny? asked Evelyn.

'What's he like?' replied Mary Magdalene. 'Everyone always asks that, but it's really not that simple. He is all things to all people, and he can change his appearance to suit the person he is talking to. Like me. So, right now, I look like this so as be acceptable to you.'

'You mean, you can make yourself look however you want?'

'Sadly, no. Goth is about all I can do.'

'So, what do you really look like?'

'Ah, now that would be telling,' laughed Mary Magdalene.

Adam scrutinised his older self. 'You can't expect me to believe that you've been sitting here, staring out of this window, for so long that you've forgotten when you first came here? What are you looking at anyway, and where's the castle?'

'Back to that again, are we? I told you, there is no castle.'

'But I walked through the castle to get here!'

'You did?' the man scrunched up his face, deep in thought. 'You know, I think I do vaguely remember there being a castle. Once upon a time. But there hasn't been a castle here for a long, long time now.'

'But you must have been here for years.'

'Could have been. Time is very strange here, almost like it's stopped; I've never really been able to work it out, seems like only a few minutes since I arrived.'

Adam though of what Evelyn had said about time being compressed. Perhaps that could explain the old man's confusion. But he was still perplexed. He kept reminding himself that this was only a dream, he had to stay calm. 'I understand, it must be very confusing for you. What is it that you are looking at?' he asked, gesturing to the window again.

'Can't you see it,' replied the old man.

'See what?'

'The one shed, at the bottom of the garden, with the open door.'

Adam squinted through the grimy glass. 'Oh yes, I can see it.'

'Occasionally, you can see a yellow glow coming from inside. I'm certain there's one of those ladders in there.'

'Like the one I, well, I guess we, came down to get here?'

'I was sure I'd arrived here somehow! I remember now. Yes, like that one.'

Mary Magdalene grabbed Evelyn's hand, her head pointing towards the wooden door.

'Come on, Evelyn! We're going to have so much fun together.'

Evelyn let herself be dragged along; still not entirely sure what Mary Magdalene meant by 'fun'.

'Perhaps we should go and investigate,' Adam suggested.

'That would be a good idea, yes, investigate. Why hadn't I thought of that?'

'I don't know, but I'm going to have a look. Want to come?'

'Perhaps not, my legs aren't what they used to be. But you go ahead, I'll be here when you get back.'

III

The scene: a skyscraper, clad in steel and marble, with a brand new, gleaming Boeing 837 ID-*Super* hovering alongside. Constructed to carry ten people, with a crew of four, it is the latest in inter-dimensional travel. Today, though, only one passenger is on board: an elderly gentleman, who nods to the commissionaire as he alights the plane and enters the magnificent building.

The gentleman is Oskar Oppenheimer, the wealthiest man in the world, and probably several other worlds across different dimensions; the fantastical skyscraper is the London headquarters of his company: Oppenheimer Technological Industries.

Inside, with an absence of electronic aids, and with an enormous expanse of oak panelling, the antiquated interior is the antithesis of the ultra-modern exterior. Even the late Victorian clothing Oppenheimer chooses to wear contradicts his position as the most successful individual in the technology sector. Those privileged enough to be familiar with inter-dimensional worlds would be unsure of his origins. A less advanced reality? Or a more advanced alternative, perhaps? His eccentricity makes it difficult to pin him down, and he delights in keeping people guessing, which often works in his favour, especially in business dealings.

Oppenheimer looks confused, as he takes out his gold pocket watch to check the time against that displayed above the reception desk. There are several analogue clocks, each displaying the current time in different realities, all of which he operates within. The receptionist points to the correct clock, and he smiles, holding up his hand in thanks before correcting his watch. On his way to the lift, he greets several aides, who take it in turns to brief him. But their efforts are in vain, for as soon as the lift doors open, he waves them away. He has more important matters on his mind; one hundred and eighty floors up is the office of the only person he wants to see.

The man in question is Felix Benson, senior executive, in charge of research and development. He is leading Oppenheimer's new pet project: The Oppenheimer Patent Educational and Learning System.

'So, have you managed to iron out the glitches?' asks Oppenheimer, immediately upon entering Benson's bronze walled office.

'We started working on it straight away, though I fear the fault is far more serious than we originally thought,' Benson replies, rising from his seat in deference.

Oppenheimer's old face hardens, as he takes Benson's seat behind an uncluttered, stainless-steel desk. Oppenheimer hates clutter and expects his employees to operate in a tidy and efficient manner.

'What do you mean more serious? Your people gave me assurances that the system would be one hundred percent reliable.'

'We expected it to be so. But a fault has occurred somewhere no one anticipated.'

'No one anticipated? This brings us back to the 'one hundred percent reliable' guarantee!'

'Allow me to explain.'

'Please do.' Oppenheimer leans back in Benson's enormous leather office chair, his hand gesturing for Benson to continue.

'There is no fault with the software we are using. But something is preventing our connection to the hardware.'

'Benson, what exactly is the problem? I have a great deal riding on this. Your team has already cost me a small fortune, and I had hoped to be able to sell the system by now. I will admit, so far, the only interest has been from a UK government in a slightly less advanced alternate, and they still need some convincing. But I should be able to get a sale out of them. This is one of my hardest sells yet, but we have no fall back. If this fails, I will lose a lot of money, potentially enough to bankrupt us. To bankrupt ME!' He leans forward, a determined expression on his face. 'We must be absolutely certain the system is failsafe.'

Oppenheimer rises from the seat and walks over to the window, as Benson continues nervously.

'The problem is down to compatibility. The hardware is not of this world, and we are finding problems when connecting it to our software, which is—'

Oppenheimer is staring out of the window, watching a wisp of golden-yellow mist rise as the doors of another inter-dimensional transporter open.

'You knew this, you should have considered this problem in the early stages.' Oppenheimer sighed. 'But I suppose I am partly to blame; I should have involved myself more. What we need to do now is figure out how to work around it.'

'Sir, when we acquired—'

'Stole,' said Oppenheimer, now looking at the forest of less important skyscrapers, stretching into the distance. 'Remember that. We stole the hardware, or system, or device, whatever you want to call it, from Benson Technological, our parallel in an alternate world. Fortunately for us, they do not yet have the capacity to travel between alternate realties. But given their speed of advancement, they soon will, and they will be wanting their hardware back.' Oppenheimer turns and bangs the desk with his fist. 'Hence why it is so important that we fix this problem, so we can rid ourselves of the device, hopefully at a profit.'

'But, Sir, when it came into our possession, we thought everything would be compatible. There should not have been a problem in the first place.'

Oppenheimer returns to his seat and stares at a still nervous Benson. 'Except there is a problem, isn't there. A major problem. So, explain it to me. Is it just a difference in technology? Or is there more to it?' Oppenheimer's eyes widen. 'You must say now, Benson. There is a lot riding on this, time as well as money.'

'The compatibility with our software is a problem, Sir, though we suspect the hardware itself may also be somewhat unreliable…'

'I thought as much. Come on, out with it. We must get this cleared up as soon as possible. The customer has been patient, but we cannot keep them waiting much longer.'

'We have always called it hardware, Sir, but having worked with it I am more inclined to refer to it as an entity.'

'An entity? You mean a living organism?'

'We assumed there was some form of machine or computer inside the metal cube, but since we could not get inside, we could never be sure. After working with it, I am beginning to suspect it is alive. Either that, or an extremely sophisticated computer, though we have no idea what the original purpose of such a machine could have been.'

'No, we don't, except as a form of mind control, I suppose.'

'See, we assumed we could make use of it—'

'As an educational tool, to help people learn, yes, I know.' Oppenheimer sighs. 'Quite a novel idea really, I'm surprised no one else has taken it up.'

'True, Sir, but if I can get back to what I was saying? Over the past few weeks, it has been behaving as though it has a mind of its own; it seems to know we are connecting it to our software, and keeps changing the way it works, rebelling against our efforts to use it.

Currently, it seems to be stuck in some sort of religious, biblical mode. And—'

'Yes?'

'The books work well, there is no problem with those. But the main ladders...well, the system appears to be reading the mind of the user, digging into their subconscious and creating scenarios based on their thoughts and memories.'

'It's reading minds! Interesting...but how are we correcting it?'

'Well, we have introduced dampeners to the software, which should keep it under control. We don't want a repeat of the other night, the subjects could not awaken or escape from their dreams, it was very strange.'

Oppenheimer smiles as he thinks. 'Good, let us hope that has solved the problem. We cannot allow such a thing to happen when it is in service, the consequences would be truly disastrous for the company. But try to preserve the mind reading part. It may be useful for a later project.' Oppenheimer pauses for a moment. 'So, I trust—'

Benson interjects. 'I assure you, Mr Oppenheimer, we are working nonstop on this project, and have solved every problem as soon as it has appeared—'

Oppenheimer finishes his original sentence. 'So, I trust we can go ahead with the preparations?'

'Yes, we can. Definitely,' replies Benson, nodding.

'So, what plans do you have in place? We have allowed thousands of people in the alternate to experience this project, but no evaluations of the experience have been conducted. If we are going to be ready, we must press on.'

'We have pre-empted your concern, Sir, and have narrowed the subjects down to just two people. They are keen, inquisitive, and most importantly, not afraid to experiment with the system. We will inform them of the main purpose of the dreams, then allow them to continue using the system, but in a more constructive way. We have already programmed the system to allocate mentors.'

'So, you can simulate how we intend the system to work?'

'A dry run, you could call it. And we have decided not to tell them about the recent glitches.'

'Or else they would never volunteer.'

'Yes. They also work for their government. If these two employees have already experienced it, hopefully they will recommend it to others.'

'Excellent! What of the others, will they still be able to use it?'

'We will change the music track and play it at a slightly different time.'

'That should deter most of them.' Oppenheimer relaxes in his seat. 'It seems you have things under control. I will give you one month to continue testing. Then we must look at a release date.'

IV

Evelyn never did find out Mary Magdalene's plans. Nor did Adam report back to his older self. Their dreams suddenly stopped, and on opening their eyes the radio was playing a different tune. That worried Adam, as did the fact that Evelyn was absent from work for the next three days. He tried calling her, but both her mobile and landline went straight to answerphone. Even his texts and social media messages went unanswered. He thought of asking if she had called in sick, but that would draw attention to their close friendship, which they had wanted to keep secret.

'I've been trying to call,' he said, when she finally returned to work. 'Didn't you see the messages? I was beginning to worry.'

'Sorry,' replied Evelyn. 'Jo wasn't well, I had to look after her.'

'And the messages? Surely you got those?'

'My battery went flat, and I didn't have my charger. I read them this morning, but I knew I'd be seeing you today.'

Adam thought the excuse was a little strange, given that she always had a charger in her bag. And her mentioning Jo sounded strangely familiar. He let it rest, instead turning their conversation to the dreams.

'So, it was the same for you too,' he said, on hearing that her dream had also suddenly stopped. 'I thought we said we would give it a rest for a while?'

'We did, but I couldn't resist, and neither could you by the sound of it?'

'Sounds like we're two for a pair,' laughed Adam. 'Though at least we did it separately and not together.'

'Yeah, you're right. That lets us both off the hook.'

'So, do you think it's all over now? I tried last night, but it was a different tune again,' sighed Adam.

Evelyn sounded even more despondent; she told him she had tried it with her friend, and the result had been the same. She sounded so down, but no matter how hard he tried Adam could not think of anything to say to cheer her up.

'I wonder what made it happen in the first place?' Evelyn asked, trying to sound positive. 'I mean, it must have been an elaborate task, causing all those dreams? They seemed so real. It was like virtual reality. I asked Jo, but other than suggesting a signal in the music, she had no idea. And she's usually the technical one.'

Her friend Jo again. Adam tried to brush it aside. 'I don't know either. But it is bound to have come to the attention of the authorities, especially if others had been trying it. Like your friend for instance.' he added, trying to bring the conversation back round to Jo. He had been suspicious long enough; now he wanted to know more, especially since Evelyn had just spent the last few days with this woman. The thought that Evelyn might be a lesbian was still at the back of his mind. 'How is Jo, by the way? I hope she's feeling better. I bet she's just as pissed off as we are, that it's all finished I mean.'

'She's fine now, and yes, she's pretty annoyed about it.'

'Why don't we all meet up sometime?' he asked. 'I've never met Jo. I've met all the others, but not her. It would be great for us all to get together, you've mentioned her so many times.'

'Oh, we will,' was her reply. 'She's a bit on the shy side, so it might be difficult for her. But you're right, we should all meet up, sometime.'

Evelyn's attempt at deflection only fuelled Adam's suspicion. Although, of course, there could be another explanation for her not wanting him to meet Jo…maybe Evelyn wanted to keep him all to herself. The thought lifted his spirits, but before he could take the subject further, she started talking about the dreams again.

As they continued chatting, Adam contemplated his persistent concerns about Jo. Perhaps it was just jealousy. Even if Evelyn was in a lesbian relationship, she was still warm towards him and occasionally receptive to his shows of affection, so obviously what they had was more than a friendship. Perhaps she was keeping him on the backburner, a fall back, should she and Jo split? Stop it, he told himself. If he kept going along this train of thought, he would be pondering possibilities all day! He needed a distraction. Tea! Yes, tea was a good idea. The two of them had been working all morning after all, they deserved a break. And that way, when they were alone in the canteen, he could come straight out and ask about her and Jo. At least then he would know where he stood.

'Fancy a cup of tea?' he asked.

Evelyn's face lit up at his suggestion. 'Good idea,' she said.

'Right you are,' he replied. 'I'll just deal with this email while you finish what you're doing.'

Evelyn was tidying away some papers when Adam called her over.

'Hey, look at this: it says the dreams resume tonight, usual station, but a different time.'

'Are you sure?' asked Evelyn, pushing him aside to get a better view of the message. She was silent for a moment as she read the message. 'Wait…who's it from?'

'I don't recognise the address,' Adam shrugged, gesturing to the sender's details.

Evelyn's expression became confused. 'Wait, I do. Oppenheimer Educational. At school they provided all the stationery, even some of the computer software, if I remember correctly.'

'But why would they contact me, us? Are we the only ones?'

'I don't know. But, somehow, they know about us and the dreams. To be honest, I don't really care who they are, if it's true…ooh, I just want it to be tonight already!'

Adam carefully leant over the cliff's edge. The glow of the ladder became brighter. It was directly below them. 'We must be absolutely barking mad doing this,' he exclaimed, looking back at Evelyn, who was stood behind him, 'I know the email said to try tonight, but I didn't think it would be like this!'

'Me neither,' agreed Evelyn, staring at the openness in front of them.

'It's certainly similar, different music and time yes, but the same golden glow; the same ladders. But this is definitely not the library; it looks more dangerous than anything we've done before.' Adam twisted around, dangling his leg towards the ladder.

'Be careful,' gasped Evelyn, stretching out her hand in support.

Adam missed his footing and quickly hauled himself back on to the cliff's edge. 'We'll break our necks trying to do this. This isn't adventure, this is suicide.'

'Hold my hand as you step onto to the ladder,' said Evelyn. 'I'll hold you steady. Then, when you're safely secure and facing the right way round, you can help me down.'

'Okay,' replied Adam.

She watched as he nervously stepped on to the ladder, then gasped as the ladder slid to one side, before collapsing into the abyss at the base of the cliff. She tightened her hand around his, catching his other arm with her free hand before he had the chance to follow the ladder downwards.

'Well, it's definitely not going to work now,' she said, hauling him up.

Adam stared in shock at the empty space where the ladder had been. 'Agreed. No use hanging around here now, we might as well wake up,' he said, watching the yellow glow turn into a mist before finally disappearing.

'That's one option,' said Evelyn, looking at the expanse of moorland behind them. She pointed into the distance. 'Or, we could go that way, see what we find.'

'Could do, I guess. I bet we won't find much, though, not in this wilderness, surely?'

'I suppose you're right, we had better wake up. We can try again tomorrow night…if there is a tomorrow night. I guess whoever told us to try tonight didn't expect it to be like this.'

'That's what I'm thinking,' said Adam. 'Take me back to the library any day!'

He took one final look over the cliff's edge. The ground moved. Suddenly the cliff was crumbling away beneath him. Unable to reach him in time, Evelyn looked on in horror as the cliff gave way, taking Adam with it. Or so she thought. Seconds later, her eyes widened in amazement. Adam had reappeared, apparently suspended in mid-air.

Adam looked down, and then back to Evelyn. 'What the…' he exclaimed.

'What on earth,' gasped Evelyn, as Adam steadied himself. They stared at one another, neither of them knowing what to think, Adam floating in mid-air while Evelyn stood on what remained of the cliff.

Eventually, Adam broke the silence. 'I have no idea what just happened, but at least I'm still alive.'

'Perhaps there's some sort of failsafe, to prevent us from coming to any harm, like before?'

'Well, if that's true, it obviously works.'

Evelyn was impressed by Adam's courage. If the same thing had happened to her, she would have dived back onto the safety of the cliff. But there he was, just floating, slowly getting used to standing on thin air.

'Come on over, Evelyn, I think it'll be okay,' he said, beckoning with his outstretched hand.

Evelyn looked down, then back to him.

'It will be okay. Trust me.'

Without saying a word, Evelyn reached out and took his hand. Gripping it tight, she closed her eyes and carefully stepped over the edge. Next thing she knew, she was standing alongside Adam.

'See, I told you it would be alright,' he said reassuringly, smiling.

Evelyn looked about her in wonder. 'I know you did, but…wow…what an experience.' She carefully tilted her head downwards, but the sight of the long drop overwhelmed her, and she wrapped her arm around Adam's waist. 'This will take some getting used to,' she whispered nervously.

Adam countered by placing his arm around her. It felt good: they hadn't been this close since the old house, which felt like an eternity ago. But the context was all wrong, and he knew they couldn't stand there forever. 'Well, shall we explore?' he suggested.

'What, walk on thin air?' asked Evelyn apprehensively. 'Are you joking?

'Well, we haven't fallen yet. Might as well give it a go.'

Admiring Adam's nerve, Evelyn looked down. 'Alright. We move together, okay? I'm still nervous about this.'

'Don't worry, we'll go together,' replied Adam.

Then, with their arms still tightly wrapped around each other's waists, they nervously took a step forward. It felt strange, walking with nothing beneath them, but after a while they both felt confident enough to let go of each other and continue separately. A few minutes later, Evelyn suggested they stop walking, and simply think about moving forward. Being more experienced when it came to the dreams, and more adventurous in general, she was willing to throw caution to the wind and allow their imaginations to take over. It was only a dream after all, what harm could come of it? Besides, they could always just wake themselves up if any danger presented itself. That was, if it worked…given her last experience in the cellar, she was secretly worried that waking up might not be an option.

Onward they travelled, gliding over fields, woodland, and the occasional hamlet. Soon, they came across a dirt track, busy with people and their horses and carts. Everyone appeared to be travelling in the same direction, so Adam and Evelyn decided to follow them from above. Eventually, they arrived at a larger village, which they hovered over for a moment, watching the bustling market below them.

'Come on, let's investigate,' suggested Evelyn, pointing downwards.

'If we can get down,' replied Adam, looking slightly worried. 'If we stop thinking about being up here, we'll fall flat on our faces.'

Evelyn rolled her eyes. 'Of course we can get down, we just have to think about gently floating towards the ground.'

'Oh, right…of course…yes…sorry…didn't think of that.'

'Well, I did,' said Evelyn, in a very matter of fact way. 'Come on, Adam, let's go!'

Together, they floated down, landing out of sight under a group of trees. From the look of the villagers clothing, and the apparent absence of any modern technology, this place was clearly pre-industrial. Much to their relief, no one seemed to notice them; everyone was entirely focused on going about what was probably their weekly business.

'Where shall we start?' Adam asked, looking at the scene before them.

Evelyn pointed to a bench, which lay beneath the shade of an oak tree, and proposed they take a break while they decided what to do next. 'It will give us a chance to soak up the atmosphere,' she said, as they took their seats.

The two of them sat for several minutes, watching people bartering; trading their livestock for produce or services. The rural hustle and bustle was exactly what one would expect from a small open-air market.

'You'd have thought someone would have noticed two very out of place strangers by now…' Adam wondered aloud, eyeing the miscellany of traders before them. The squealing of a sow being dragged towards the stall opposite drowned out Evelyn's reply. 'What was that?' Adam asked, sickened by the sight of the animal's throat being slit by the stall holder's sharp knife.

'I said, no one will notice,' came a male voice from beside him. Adam jumped, rapidly turning around to see who had joined them. But to his horror, he saw no third person. Evelyn had been replaced.

'What…what happened to Eve?' was all he could manage, as he stared at the stranger next to him.

'Do not worry, she will be safe,' assured the newcomer: a man dressed in a white robe. 'We have placed her in another dream for now, but she will be returning.'

'Wait…what? You mean…you can control the dreams?' Adam was still in a state of shock.

'No. I am here to speak with you.' The man's voice was deep and authoritative.

'Who are you?' asked Adam.

'I represent the controllers of the dreams.'

'Okay…' replied Adam shakily. He was slowly beginning to calm down. 'So, there is someone who controls the dreams, someone who isn't you. But you are this person's representative?' The man nodded. Adam continued. 'Right. So, I guess maybe you know what these dreams are about? Do you? How do they work? Also, what happened to the library?

'Too many questions,' said the man, shaking his head. 'Though I expected nothing less. Your inquisitiveness is the very reason why you and Evelyn have been chosen—'

Adam cut him off. 'Chosen? What do you mean by chosen? And who are you?'

The man held up both hands, palms facing Adam, gesturing for him to be patient. 'Please. You are so eager. Allow me to explain. We are the people controlling the library—'

'But—'

The man gestured for silence again. 'There is so much to tell you, much of which you will not understand completely. I will try to clarify things where possible. Adam, we are an organisation working in conjunction with your government, currently experimenting on the potential for dreams to be used as a form of education. The library—'

'This is ridiculous! It's all so farfetched,' complained Adam, glaring at the man.

'Patience. Let me continue. I cannot tell you which government department we are working with, and yes, I admit, it does sound farfetched. Even I do not fully understand everything. What I do know is that this technology was introduced by people from an alternate reality. I take it you have heard of alternate realities?'

'You mean, as in layers of alternate worlds, existing simultaneously? But that has always been just speculation—'

'Quite. As I said, much of this will be difficult to comprehend.'

'Quite,' replied Adam, sarcastically. He sighed. He might as well play along; a few farfetched answers were better than no answers. 'What were you saying about education?'

'Education is the main purpose of the library. When you fall into the dream state, your subconscious is carried to a different reality. And in that reality, in that library, you are encouraged to learn.'

'The books?'

'Yes, the books. As you will have noticed, each time you open one, you are able to experience the subject of that book. So far, you have only investigated the fiction section. Now, imagine what knowledge could be attained if you were to explore the non-fiction section?'

'That does make sense, I can see how that would be a useful tool. But what about the main ladders? They don't take you into books…'

'No, but they encourage you to explore, as you and Evelyn have done. Exploration is an important part of learning.'

'But what happened this time, with the cliff edge? It scared the life out of me!'

'Ah, that was by design: it was a test, to see how you would react. You soon worked it out, both of you. That is the reason you have been chosen to carry on testing the system. Of all the people we surveyed, it was Evelyn who was the most experienced, and more crucially, the most adventurous and determined subject.'

'So…Evelyn was chosen because she is the most likely to explore, and make the most out of the system?'

'That is correct. You are learning the system too and learning quickly. In the case of the cliff, it was you who was not afraid to stand on nothing but air; not many would have been brave enough to walk over a cliff edge like you did. Together, you will make a good team.'

'But we found out about the standing on air thing by accident—'

'Yes, but did you turn back? That is the key difference. Believe me, most would have given up at the first hurdle; taken to the fields in search of sanctuary or woken themselves up, writing off the dream as a bad experience. But you two? You both pressed on, hence why you are here.'

'To be honest, we weren't sure if we would be able to use waking up as a means of escape. During our last episodes we had both experienced problems with waking ourselves up; Evelyn was terrified when she found out she couldn't escape the cellar. And then, after a while, both our dreams stopped, abruptly.'

'Ah, yes, your last experiences…nothing to be concerned about, the system was…' he paused in thought. 'That is…we were undertaking maintenance that night, so we closed down the system, to prevent anyone from becoming trapped in their dreams.'

'But those dreams, they were quite strange, nothing like what we'd been used to. They were more psychological, more disturbing.'

'Again, that would be down to the changes in the system during maintenance. Rest assured everything has now been returned to normal; there will be no repeat.'

'That's good to know. So…we passed the test then?' asked Adam, trying to move the conversation along.

'Of course. That is why we have allowed you to continue this evening.'

'But what about Eve? You said she would come back.'

'She will return. Currently, she is being briefed by one of my colleagues.'

'Right...but, you said allowed...what about the others? We have been chosen over hundreds, if not thousands, of people to continue, right? How will you stop others from entering the dreams?'

'We have considered that. As you are aware, we have changed the music track, which is now played at a ten-thirty. Though we cannot stop others from entering the dreams, we are hopeful that few will discover the changes.'

'And what about Eve and I testing the system? How will that work? Will you be monitoring us?'

'Not exactly. We will not be watching you, which I believe is what you are referring to. Instead, we will contact you from time to time, to ask how you are finding the system. Do not forget, the dreams are intended to be educational, so we expect you to make greater use of the books in the library, especially those from the non-fiction section.'

'But what about Evelyn's friend? She's used the system quite a lot, alone and with Evelyn.'

'Ah yes, Joanne. We did consider Joanne. She is very astute—'

'She worked out that the signal was buried in the music track—'

'Quite. But no. In the end, we decided she would be too much of a distraction for Evelyn to experience the system properly.'

'In what way?' Adam asked, hoping he would find out more about Evelyn and Jo.

'I do not know the details. All I know is that those monitoring the subjects advised against her being involved.'

'Perhaps I should ask Evelyn myself?'

'Yes, perhaps. I am not here to solve your personal conundrums.' The man suddenly looked upwards, then looked back at Adam. 'You are free to use the system. I will be in touch.'

The man in the white robe looked upwards again, and instantly disappeared.

Adam sat on the bench, looking down at his hands, trying to process what had just happened. A short distance away, a yellow mist formed, and as Adam looked up, out walked Evelyn.

'Welcome back!' Adam smiled, standing to greet her.

'Have you heard the news?' shrieked Evelyn running towards him. 'It's back! The library, everything,' she continued, hugging Adam tightly.

'Yeah,' replied Adam, before releasing her.

'Who briefed you?'

'A man in white robe.'

'Was it a youngish man? Good looking, looks like he works out a lot?'

'Yes,' confirmed Adam, smiling. 'Though I couldn't say whether he was good looking, he wasn't my type. His voice didn't really fit his appearance though…he had a deep, sort of been-around-since-the-dawn-of-time voice.'

'Sounds like Saint Peter,' said Evelyn. 'You remember? I told you about him. Unlucky. I got Mary Magdalene, she's way more fun. Did you get a guided tour?'

'What? No…there was no tour, just this man talking to me.'

'Oh, guess I'm still Mary's favourite then,' giggled Evelyn, still brimming with excitement.

'Must be,' replied Adam dolefully, jealous of Evelyn's special treatment. 'What was it like?' he continued, trying to show enthusiasm.

'It was brilliant. Were you told this is all from an alternate reality?'

'Yeah, something like that.'

'You should have seen it, Adam. Mary took me through all these different rooms, with hundreds of people working at workstations; the computers were out of this world! Which makes sense I guess,' she laughed. 'Then she led me into this gigantic chamber, with this massive silver cube hooked up to the central computer. Mary never said what was in the cube, but I assume it must be the heart of the system. I was going to ask but she whisked me away. Perhaps that's the most secret part of it all…'

'Was it like the silver cube in the cellar?'

'Yeah, kind of. It was much bigger though.'

'Did she say who they were, and what the purpose of it all was? I was told it was all for educational purposes.'

'I asked her, and she said the system was being developed as method of teaching. They're far more advanced than us; they've learnt how to jump between different realities, Adam, it's incredible! Apparently, if the dream system is successful, they hope to introduce it to other worlds, worlds like ours.'

'I only hope that's true. For some reason, at the back of my mind, I feel like there's something sinister about all this. Think about it: if they can educate with this thing, they can also brainwash—'

'Yeah, yeah, I know,' said Evelyn, trying to dispel his negativity. 'But it's so exciting, though, isn't it?'

'Did Mary explain how it all works? Saint Peter was a bit cagey about the details; said he didn't fully understand everything.'

Evelyn took a deep breath. 'Well, we know it's all from an alternate reality; when we enter the library, that is one reality, and each time we use a ladder it takes us to another reality. It's like layers of different worlds, all side by side, or on top of one another. Now, the books are slightly different. They are connected to the main system, hence all those computers. Complicated, I know, but Mary said that was the easiest way to explain it.'

'So, what happened the other night? I was told they closed the system down, for maintenance or something.'

'That's right. As I said, the cube Mary showed me was like the one in the cellar. When I told her what had happened, she could only assume it was part of the maintenance work. Their cube gave off a brilliant heat and started vibrating too, same as the one I saw.'

'Seems like too much of a coincidence to me. Did she tell you why you couldn't escape?'

'No one could get out of the dream, because of the maintenance. That's when they shut the whole system down. Everything suddenly stopped. But hey, it's working now!' finished Evelyn. 'Great, isn't it?'

With Evelyn in such a jubilant mood, Adam decided to take this opportunity to ask about her friend, Jo. 'I asked if your friend would be joining us,' he said. 'But apparently, she would have been too much of a distraction for you…shame really, it would have been nice to have her with us.'

'Ah, yes,' replied Evelyn cagily.

'Strange really, I thought you were the best of friends, and made a great team?'

'I'm not sure what they meant about her being a distraction. She was just in it for the fun; she isn't quite as adventurous as me. Like, when we were in New York, I wanted to visit the art galleries and museums, but she only wanted to visit the shops…maybe that's why they didn't choose her.'

'I see,' said Adam, pleased that Evelyn and Jo's relationship was not as simple as he had assumed.

'Jo and I are best mates; we share the same interests and all that. But I can understand why they wouldn't want her with me, with us.'

'She wouldn't have taken it seriously enough,' continued Adam.

'Yeah, that's probably it.'

'To be honest, I got the impression you two were more than just friends. I don't mind—'

Evelyn cut him short. 'No! It's nothing like that! It's just that when we're together we're—'

'Inseparable?'

'Exactly,' replied Evelyn, thankful for Adam's interpretation.

'So, you're not—'

'Definitely not,' laughed Evelyn. 'I like boys too much.' Then, on seeing Adam's relief, 'You weren't jealous, were you?'

'No,' replied Adam, his face reddening.

'You were! I can see you were.'

'Okay, perhaps I was a bit jealous. I was hoping we were—'

'Going to be a couple?' smiled Evelyn, being her usual upfront self.

Her answer emboldened Adam, 'Well, yes.'

'We do make a good team; share the same interests. And you're a good kisser', she laughed. 'We are going to be spending a lot of time together, in the dreams and all that...' she paused, deep in thought. 'To be honest, I suppose I was secretly hoping the same.'

Adam smiled. 'So, we're on the same wavelength. A proper team. Together.'

Evelyn took his hand. 'Together.'

Adam wrapped his arms around her. 'But why now? After all this time?'

'I was frightened,' whispered Evelyn, nervously.

'Frightened? Of what?' asked Adam, tightening his arms around her.

'I've never had a boyfriend before. Everyone I've been out with has only wanted me for one thing.'

'Like those guys in the office? You know I'm not like them, Evelyn.'

'I know. That's why I like you so much. You're so sweet, I could love you! I…' Evelyn stopped. 'I…I love you, Adam.'

'I love you too, Eve. That's why I've always stayed with you,' replied Adam, relieved that they were of the same mind. He felt Evelyn pull away slightly from his embrace, and he looked down at her as she looked up at him, her eyes sparkling. As he leant his face towards her, she slid her hand behind his neck and kissed him on the lips. They remained locked in each other's embrace for some time until, eventually, Evelyn released her hold.

'What do we do now?' she asked, holding his hands.

'What we're here to do, I guess: explore,' shrugged Adam. 'But not here,' he added, glancing at the bloodied remains of the sow on the stall holder's floor. 'This place gives me the creeps.'

'Okay, let's explore somewhere else.'

'What, another village?' asked Adam, looking curiously at the sparkle in Evelyn's eyes.

'Or we could use the ladder,' said Evelyn, with a broad grin.

'What ladder? Where is it? Did Miss Magdalene tell you where to find it?'

'We've been through this, Adam!' she laughed, playfully hitting him on the shoulder. 'You just have to think of it, silly!' She grinned. 'Guess this means you still need me around. God only knows what would happen if you were here all by yourself. Come on, let's think of the ladder, together.'

V

'Game to Miss Williams. Miss Williams leads two games to one in the final set,' announced the umpire.

'I've never been to Wimbledon before,' said Adam, continuing to eat through his bowlful of strawberries and cream.

'Me neither,' replied Evelyn, licking the last of the cream off her fingers. 'Always been too expensive, not that I'm into tennis that much.'

'Fancy the ladder bringing us here,' laughed Adam. 'And on the day of the women's final, as well.'

'Perhaps it's a reward for our dedication,' Evelyn shrugged, smiling. 'Perhaps the powers that be like us so much that they decided to reward us with this.'

'Perhaps.'

'The Wimbledon final; strawberries and cream; a nice cloudy day to prevent us from being burnt to a cinder…I mean, what more could we ask for?' Evelyn smiled, popping the last of her strawberries into her mouth.

'True, I bet those strawberries cost a small fortune—'

'Undoubtedly. But we are in the Royal Box, they are probably thrown in for free.'

'Most likely,' said Adam, examining the dignitaries around them.

'Have you noticed all the strange looks we've been getting,' whispered Evelyn.

'Bet they don't get to sit alongside a couple of goths very often,' snorted Adam, catching the eye of an elegant middle-aged woman, who was sitting a couple of rows down.

'I think you've pulled,' giggled Evelyn, hiding her face with her hand.

'Looks like it, and I bet she's loaded too.'

'I'll scratch both of your eyes out if either of you make a move,' warned Evelyn.

'Who's the jealous one now,' chuckled Adam.

'So? You belong to me now. Nobody's touching you,' said Evelyn, sitting up and grabbing his hand to make her point.

'I better be careful then, looks like I've got myself a bunny boiler.' He winked at her.

'Too true, mister, you're mine now, so don't forget it,' laughed Evelyn, poking him in the ribs.

Adam wrapped his arm around Evelyn. 'Changing the subject, what shall we do when the match is finished? I was thinking of calling it a night and getting some proper sleep.'

'Good idea. Tomorrow's Sunday so why don't we go shopping, then make a proper start on the dreams tomorrow night?'

'Perfect,' said Adam. 'Our first proper shopping expedition together.'

That night, Adam slept on the sofa in the lounge, while Evelyn used the only bedroom in his Hampstead flat. They woke up late, tired after their long night of exploring, and Adam prepared breakfast while Evelyn used the shower. After a delicious full English, with ample supplies of tea and chatter, they set off hand in hand, sometimes arm in arm, towards the city. They had already decided which shops they wanted to visit, and spent the day browsing goth boutiques and wandering through the sci-fi and fantasy sections of numerous London bookshops.

At five o'clock they arrived back at Evelyn's town house, where they finished off the pizza's they had bought on the way home. As they ate, they surmised what the library would bring them that night. Visits to exotic places? Or perhaps tours of strange and surreal landscapes? Whatever lay ahead, they could not wait to turn on the radio.

'I guess we have about four hours until dream time,' said Evelyn, as she sat curled up on the sofa in the front room.

'We've got time for a *Lord of the Rings* film,' suggested Adam, 'or perhaps two or three episodes of *X-Files*.'

Evelyn smiled at his suggestions. 'Or a couple of *Matrix's*,' said Evelyn, looking at her DVD collection.

'Four hours is a long time to kill,' sighed Adam.

'What shall we do then?' asked Evelyn. 'Flicking through Sky channels sounds good, but I must admit, I'm getting tired of that now. And I've seen all of my DVDs, most of them umpteen times.'

'Can you think of anything better to do?' asked Adam.

Evelyn sat for a while in contemplation. Shyly, she looked at Adam, then looked away, then looked again. Finally, she summoned up her courage and climbed on top of him. 'My double bed's more than big enough for the two of us,' she said huskily, the torn knees of her jeans rubbing against Adam's legs. 'Plenty big enough for a few hours of fun,' she added, brushing her lips against his forehead.

Adam smiled. 'Well, I suppose that way there's no chance of us missing the radio.'

'Exactly.'

'What are we waiting for, then? Shall we head upstairs?'

Evelyn smiled seductively, lifting herself off him and entwining her fingers in his.

'You know, when we're in the library, we could look through the books, see what takes our fancy,' he suggested, as Evelyn pulled him up off the sofa.

'I was thinking the same,' Evelyn replied, as they walked towards the door.

'Fifty Shades?'

Evelyn stopped and smirked. 'Well, that would be good…but I was thinking of something better.'

'What could be better?' laughed Adam.

'Karma Sutra?' replied Evelyn, with a mischievous grin. 'Wouldn't that be an idea? After all, we were instructed to investigate the textbooks, weren't we?

'We were, indeed,' grinned Adam. 'How about we get some practice in while we wait?'

Evelyn's eyes sparkled. 'Always better to be prepared.'

The Royal Birth

The King had decreed that the imminent royal birth would be marked by a public holiday, and when the happy day arrived, everyone in the Kingdom rejoiced. Throughout the day, inns and ale houses were awash with people celebrating; the Royal Bakery had prepared a feast of delicacies to be distributed amongst the well-wishers, and fireworks had been set up in the palace grounds, ready and waiting to light up the night sky. Everyone was happy. Everyone. Except the King.

At first, when a servant had presented him with the new-born babe, he had been jubilant. But as he pulled back the cotton shroud, to reveal the tiny human wrapped inside, his look of excitement had turned to one of horror. The King and the Queen were Caucasian; pure. But the baby…the baby was half-caste; more yellow than white. The doctors were quick to suggest that the infant's colouring could be the result of jaundice.

'The child's yellow skin could be the sign of a serious complication,' one had said, before insisting that the babe be properly examined. Though thankful for their promptness, the King was not completely assured. He was aware of the rumours that his Queen was sharing her bed with others, though he had always brushed them off as court gossip, put about by female courtiers who were jealous that he had chosen a beautiful young princess from another Kingdom over one of them or one of their daughters. Now, he was no longer sure.

Tests showing the baby to be in perfect health confirmed the rumours. Despite the child's appearance being a closely guarded secret, those who knew the colour of the royal baby could tell that the King was looking for the one who had dared to share an intimate liaison with his Queen. At court, the King scrutinised and examined, watching the courtiers body language, looking for signs of a guilty conscience. All to no avail: none showed any signs of guilt, or concealment of guilt. It was a fruitless exercise in the first place, for all those in court were white. He would have to look elsewhere.

The King instructed the Court Prosecutor to investigate the rumours. Discretely, for when the culprit was found the King intended to impose punishment himself, avoiding a trial and the possibility of the perpetrator going free. His anger had been roused and everyone was afraid, avoiding eye contact: even if innocent, any sign of fear could be misconstrued as guilt. They all feared the King's own style of merciless justice.

It was time for the royal christening, and the King's advisors had recommended another public holiday. The public had greatly enjoyed the celebrations for the child's birth; they felt another similar day to mark the christening would enhance the King's standing. An honours list was also suggested, not just of favoured courtiers, but also including members of the community, who were not usually included in the King's annual birthday list. And so, the list was drawn: inn keepers; blacksmiths; store holders; teachers…people from almost every walk of life were included. The public were delighted; never had commoners been recognised in such a prestigious fashion.

The preparations were almost in place. But just as the final names were being added to the list, the Court Prosecutor whispered one name in the King's ear: Zhu Fu, the man in charge of the palace grounds. The King looked to the Prosecutor. The Prosecutor nodded. The

King instantly had a plan, and Zhu Fu's name was placed on to the list.

The day of the christening arrived, and everyone celebrated once again. After a grand service in the cathedral came the distribution of honours, presented in the royal throne room. First were the Lords and Ladies, then senior members of the court and their families. Next, the members of the public. Those in high standing first: the doctors, lawyers, and such like. Then, finally, the honours for those in the lower echelons of society, to be presented by the Queen.

Last on the list was Zhu Fu, who was honoured for keeping the royal gardens in fine order. The King looked across at the Prosecutor, and the Prosecutor nodded his head towards the Chinese man. The King watched as Zhu Fu knelt before the Queen. And as they held each other in a stare, Fu lowered his head for the Queen to place a sash around his neck. The King watched with intensity as Fu rose and the Queen smiled, congratulating him with a shake of the hand. Suddenly, there came a large gasp from the court, as the Queen ran her hand up Fu's arm before breaking royal protocol and embracing him tenderly. A loud 'ahem' from the Chief Usher broke their entanglement. As soon as they had parted, Zhu Fu fled from the court, back to his humble quarters next to the royal greenhouses.

Astonished chatter followed, and the King had his answer. For him, there was no doubt that Zhu Fu was the father of the royal child. The King took the Prosecutor to one side, and for several minutes they engaged in quiet conference. They parted and nodded to one another before the Prosecutor hurried from the royal throne room. The remaining proceedings were a sombre affair. After the impromptu embrace, everyone could detect an atmosphere between the King and Queen, though only a few knew the cause. The royal baby was always covered, and the infant's skin colour remained a secret. Even the Queen's maids were sworn to silence, as were the courtiers, and they all kept that silence, knowing they would suffer the pain of death for breaking it.

By the time the royal dinner came around that evening, the mood had lightened. With enough food to feed the entire kingdom, and with the best entertainers brought in from several realms, everyone enjoyed the banquet. Mid-way through, the King rose and made a surprise announcement. Immediately following the celebration, he stated that he would be departing for his brother's castle, where they would make plans for a four-day hunting party.

The King spent that night at his brother's castle, leaving the Queen alone with only the royal baby for company. The next morning, he set out on his expedition. They caught six stags that day, along with countless rabbits and pheasants, more than enough for another banquet that night in the royal tent. The second day started equally well. The sun shone, the temperature was fair, and by midday they had caught another two stags. Come mid-afternoon, the King's party was joined by the Court Prosecutor.

'My king, you must return immediately,' he told the King.

The returning party rode swiftly, and it was early evening when the King, the Prosecutor and a small contingent of the King's personal guard arrived back at the palace, where they were met by the Sergeant at Arms. Rather than leading the King and his troops into the palace, the Prosecutor and Sergeant led them to the royal greenhouses, where a light could be seen shining in Zhu Fu's small cottage nearby. Holding his finger to his lips, the King watched as the Prosecutor crept towards the door and carefully lifted the latch. What had started as muffled cries within became louder as the door was opened. The Prosecutor stepped aside, allowing the King to see inside the house; to see his Queen sitting astride Zhu Fu on the bed.

Knowing the strength of the King's rage, the Prosecutor rushed forward to take charge of the situation, only to find his way barred by the King's arm. Wanting first to observe the spectacle, the King held his men back until he was ready to make his move. He and his troops watched the Queen's excitement growing as she performed on top of Zhu Fu. Some few minutes passed before the King made his move.

It was as the Queen was reaching her peak that the King allowed his men to step forward, his expression one of cold fury as two of his guards hooked their hands under the Queen's arms, lifting her off Zhu Fu. Shocked and wracked with guilt, both the Queen and Zhu Fu remained wide eyed and silent as they contemplated the fate that awaited them. When the guards presented the naked Queen to the King, he stared into her eyes, his face expressionless, looking for some explanation of her infidelity. No one spoke. Then, quite suddenly, the King looked up, motioning for the guards to take his wife away. He watched coldly as she was led, still naked, to her imprisonment and almost certain death, before turning his attention towards Zhu Fu.

Zhu Fu shook with fear on seeing the King draw his dagger, knowing his death was imminent. With the

King's one hand pushing down on him, Zhu Fu cringed as the King's other hand lifted his semi-erect member, closing his eyes in terror as the cold metal of the dagger drew nearer.

'Not now, my king,' exclaimed the Prosecutor. 'There will be time later for retribution. First, there must be a trial.'

A few days later, the necessary trial was held, and a shocked public learned the full extent of the Queen's secret liaisons. The Prosecutor had been thorough in his investigations, and the crowd stood aghast as he read out the names of two of the King's guardsmen, a footman, the royal coach driver, and Zhu Fu, all of whom stood in the dock, their heads bowed as the charges were read aloud. All were poor and did not have the funds to finance a strong defence; it would not have made a difference in any case. The evidence was overwhelming. One by one, witnesses were brought forward to testify their suspicions about the Queen's adulterous affairs. The trial was brief and the punishment absolute: execution, on the grounds of treason and offences against the King.

In a separate trial, because she had admitted her crime, claiming she had been coerced by the Queen after a heaving drinking session into sharing her intimacy, a chambermaid was also found guilty. Her honesty, and female sex, convinced the court to give her a more lenient sentence: banishment, rather than execution.

The Queen was also subject to a separate trial, where the full details of her adultery were again read aloud to the court. When the Prosecutor came to the case of Zhu Fu, and explained that Zhu Fu, not the King, was the father of the royal baby, the female courtiers screamed and spat at the Queen in disgust. The Queen could not present evidence in her defence. She had no answer to the charges, standing in silence with her head bowed as her sentence was passed.

It was a crisp winter's morning on the day the executions were to be carried out, and thousands had turned out to watch the spectacle. Many booed and jeered as the Queen was led through the streets and onto the scaffold; some women wept when she was refused the dignity of a blindfold. The Queen had to watch as, one by one, her lovers were forced to suffer a slow and painful death. Their un-tethered legs kicked in the air as the noose slowly tightened around their necks, garrotting the life out of them. Worse still, the crowd gasped as the hangman misjudged the weight of the royal coachman and his hefty body crashed to the wooden floor with a loud thud, his head having been wrenched from his shoulders.

The hangings were a bloody mess, but they were quick and merciful compared to what awaited Zhu Fu. He was to be the star of the show. Before he was led onto the scaffold, a block was placed in front of the Queen, so she would have a clear view of her child's father's final moments. She stared at Zhu Fu as he stood before her, their eyes locked in one final look of love.

With his hands tied behind his back, Fu remained expressionless, as his breeches were pulled down to allow the executioner to castrate him with the King's dagger. Held between two guards to prevent him from collapsing in pain, Fu watched as his genitalia were held up for the crowd to see, before being tossed into a brazier. With blood already spewing onto the block, Fu was forced to kneel for the final act. The first blow of the axe missed his neck, burying itself in his back. Already crippled by the castration, Fu cried out in agony. Some in the crowd thought incompetence on the part of the executioner was to blame for the first blow missing, but soon they realised it was done by design, after the second blow also deliberately missed its target.

The crowd were beginning to shout: some willing the executioner to continue the cruel punishment; others begging for the hacking to stop and for Fu to be put out of his misery. The former won the executioner's favour, and the third blow sliced into the top of Fu's head, the ejecting blood soaking the Queen's pure white robe. Everyone could see that Fu was still alive.

The fourth blow finally struck Fu's neck, causing his head to fall forward. But it was not totally severed, and the executioner was forced to use a fifth blow to slice through the remaining strands of flesh which connected Fu's head to his body. All the while, Fu's heart continued to pump, sending strong spurts of blood from the hole which had once been his neck, drenching the Queen and all those around her. The Queen remained emotionless, as Fu's disfigured head finally fell to the wooden floor, where it remained as Fu's body was lifted from the block and unceremoniously thrown onto the growing pile of dead bodies.

Then, it was the Queen's turn, and she was led to the same place where Fu had knelt. She required no assistance, lowering her head gracefully onto the block. Everyone could feel the executioner's pain as he looked down on this beautiful young woman, whose life he was about to take. He looked to the King and the King looked away. The executioner looked back down at the Queen. Putting his axe to one side he drew his sword, and with one swift blow the Queen's head fell to the floor.

'Are you okay?' asked Francis, as he opened his eyes to see me sitting, staring at a blank wall.

'I'll be alright,' I told him, while trying to empty my mind.

'That dream again,' he asked, gently rubbing my back in concern.

'Yeah.'

'Exactly the same dream?'

'The same dream.' My name is Amber Martin and Francis is my roommate; we share a bedsit in Reading. Both of us are PhD students, currently trying to finish our doctorates at Reading University. We eat together, go out together, and occasionally sleep together; I suppose you could say we are friends with benefits. It's complicated.

'Exactly the same dream?' he repeated, climbing onto my bed to give me a hug.

'Yep, exactly the same, no different,' I replied, sighing.

'The royal birth, the hunting party, the beheadings…'

'Yes, all the same, in all their gory detail.' I was tired of his constant questioning. The same questions, every time. I knew he cared, but at the same time I was convinced he only wanted to know more of the gruesome details.

Francis counted on his fingers. 'That's the third time this week, and the tenth, no, twelfth time in total?'

'That sounds about right. But please don't keep on, it's bad enough having the dream without having to repeat the details every time.'

'Sorry. I'm just concerned, Ambs. I'm only trying to help.'

'I know you are,' I replied, gently pushing him back onto the bed, then stretching over to kiss him. 'Thanks.'

Francis pulled me so I was lying next to him, then turned on his side to face me, nuzzling my neck. Feeling his hand on my leg, I pushed him away and sat up again.

'Not now, Fran. I'm not in the mood, okay?'

'Thought it might help take your mind off things. A—'

I knew exactly what he was going to say. 'I know. A good shag. But—' I didn't really know what to say, so I leant back, kissed him again, and made my way to the door.

Sitting on the swing seat in the garden, the early morning air warm on my face, helped to soothe my troubled mind. It was three o'clock and what I needed most was a cigarette, and the tranquillity of the communal garden. I managed five minutes of quiet reflection before Francis came out to join me.

'Better now?' he asked, as I swivelled my packet of cigarettes towards him.

'A lot, thanks,' I said, watching him remove a cigarette and light it. We gently swayed back and forth on the swing seat together, enjoying our cigarettes in silence.

Francis spoke first. 'That's not the first time you've refused to make love. These dreams must be really getting to you.'

'Tell me about it.' I was too tired to talk, but I made the effort anyway. 'It must be the stress. I've only got five weeks until completion and I'm still only halfway through writing up.'

'You're probably right. I haven't even started mine yet and I'm not looking forward to it. I thought you said you were writing as you went along, to 'save yourself the stress later'?'

'I was, but things came up. I had to do a new piece of research which threw me completely; put me well behind schedule.'

'Oh yeah, I remember that.'

'That was stressful enough, suddenly having new deadlines to meet—'

He butted in and stopped me. 'You managed it though, Ambs. I wouldn't have been able to do that.'

I winked and gave him a smile. 'Good, aren't I?'

'You can say that again.' He paused and his expression became serious again. 'What are we going to do about these dreams, then?'

'I don't know.' I shrugged, taking a long drag on my cigarette. 'As I said, it's probably the stress.'

'Yes, but the same dream every time? That must mean something.'

'That's what's bugging me. The dreams are bad enough, especially the execution part, but the reoccurrence?' I took a deep breath, 'The blood and brain as the Chinese man's head is sliced open? I can even feel the sword slicing into my neck and my head hitting the floor when the Queen's executed—'

Francis held up a hand to stop me. 'Okay, okay. You've already told me the details. Every time you're like a witness repeating to a court the events of some road accident. It's as if you were there.'

'That's the frightening part.'

'Why don't you ask for an extension, extenuating circumstances or something like that?'

'I thought about it, but I can't. I checked with my supervisor and he recommended against it. But I have put on hold the article I was working on, until the PhD is all done and dusted,' I replied, taking one final drag on my cigarette before stubbing the remains out in an almost overflowing ashtray. I immediately took another from the packet; it had been a long time since I had chain smoked, but my nerves were shot to pieces.

Seeing that Francis had also finished his cigarette I passed him another. 'I'll get there.'

'Surely one of your experts could help,' he asked after a couple of long drags. 'One of them is bound to have explored the meaning of dreams, even their causes.'

The sound of the latch on the gate at the bottom of the garden stopped our conversation. There were voices approaching, and we saw Andrew and Nathan, stooping to avoid the overhanging trees as they came through. They couldn't have realised we were there because Nathan continued to screech at Andrew.

'Course you were!' came Nathan's effeminate voice.

'I told you, I was not! So, don't keep on, please!' countered Andrew, in his deeper, masculine tone.

Nathan and Andrew lived in the bedsit above us. Apparently, they had been an item for ages, but had only just recently moved in together. I had forgotten it was a Thursday…Wednesday was LGBTQ+ night at the

Equations nightclub in town; the two of them usually returned at about this time in the morning. As usual, Nathan had drunk far too much, and they were having a tiff.

'Oh, helloooo,' cooed Nathan, finally noticing us on the swing seat. 'Out a bit late, aren't we? Oh, please don't tell me we're interrupting something, you weren't about to—'

Andrew stopped him. 'Now, Nathan, behave. It's none of our business what they get up to. Come on, best we leave them to it. Anyway, you would only get jealous if you found out.'

We all knew about Nathan's crude imagination. Especially after a few drinks when the innuendo got louder and coarser.

'Sorry about that,' continued Andrew, looking apologetically at us. 'You know what he's like.'

'What he's like? What he's like! WHAT HE'S LIKE!' shouted Nathan, his voice growing louder every time. He pointed accusingly at Andrew. 'You can talk! YOU were chatting up the DJ!'

'I told you, I was not chatting up the DJ. We were talking about the music. Anyway, the DJ's a she, so I wouldn't be chatting her up, would I?'

'Any closer and you'd have been snogging her,' exclaimed Nathan.

'We had to get close, the music was so loud we couldn't hear each other.'

'That bitch would've had her tongue down your throat if I hadn't arrived.'

'Oh please, we were only talking. It's only your vivid imagination saying there was something going on. As I've said, we weren't up to anything, and if you can't trust me—'

Finally realising that he was causing a scene, Nathan opted to surrender. 'Oh, whatever.' He rolled his eyes and turned towards the house. 'Please yourself, I'm going to bed.'

As we were facing towards the garden, we could only faintly hear Nathan's grumbling as he walked into the house. I had thought Andrew was with him, until I felt a pair of hands rubbing my shoulders.

'Take no notice of him, we know how jealous he gets if he sees me talking to someone else,' Andrew sighed.

'Don't we just,' came Francis' sarcastic, mumbled reply.

Francis had never got on with Nathan or Andrew, probably because Nathan had once made a pass at him; suggested he joined them in a threesome. I had known Andrew would never have agreed to it, the thought would have appalled him, but that had not stopped

Nathan. Unfortunately, Francis tarred Andrew with the same brush, hence the reason he wanted as little to do with him as possible.

Which was just as well. While Francis was staring at the floor, randomly kicking the gravel under his feet as he smoked his cigarette, Andrew was gently massaging my shoulders. It was superb, just the tonic I needed to chase the stress away, especially when Andrew started digging his thumbs into my tensest muscles.

'It's Nathan's birthday next week,' Andrew continued.

Francis' sarcasm continued. 'Yay…'

Andrew carried on regardless. 'So, I was planning a surprise party in the VIP area at the club, that's what I was talking to the DJ about. Course, you two are invited, you're top of the list.'

As he finished speaking, I felt a jolt of elation as his hands gripped me harder.

'Hmmm,' mumbled Francis.

'Great, we'd love to come,' I replied, ignoring Francis' obvious lack of enthusiasm. 'Wouldn't we, Fran?' I said, digging my elbow into his ribs.

'Of course,' he sighed, still staring at the floor.

'Magic, I'll give you more details later,' Andrew replied, grinning.

'Super.' I smiled in contentment, still enjoying the feel of his fingers, which were now working my neck muscles. I nodded to the packet of cigarettes on the table. 'Would you like a cigarette, Andy?'

Andrew was about to answer when we heard the grinding sound of a window opening above us. Andrew immediately released his grip and we both looked up to see a semi-naked Nathan hanging out of the window.

'Are you coming or what? I'm gagging up here,' Nathan shrieked, before going back inside.

I had to smirk as Andrew muttered 'she who must be obeyed' under his breath, before going on to mimic Nathan's high pitched shrill.

'We must have our special after-clubbing shag, you know I'm not complete until we've rounded off the night properly.' Then, in his normal voice. 'I'd better go, he'll only sulk if I stay down here too long. We'd never hear the last of it. Thanks for the offer though. I've something stronger upstairs if you want some, I'll throw it down if you like?'

'Not right now,' I replied. 'But if the offer is still there for during the party…we won't be able to afford too many drinks, so a few spliffs would be a good substitute.'

'Right you are then,' replied Andrew.

He had obviously noticed that Francis was still staring at the ground, for next thing I knew I could feel a warm breath and a pair of velvety lips against my ear.

'Catch you later, babes,' he whispered.

I dared not reply, in case Francis heard, so instead I twisted my head round and kissed him on the cheek.

'Has he gone?' asked Francis, craning his head to look at the door.

'He's gone.'

'Thank God. Those two give me the creeps. Now, where were we?'

'Experts,' I said. 'There's Professor Jonson who I interviewed last year. He's done a fair bit of work in that area.'

'Oh yes, I remember you going to see him. You got on well, right? Why don't you get in touch? You've got nothing to lose; even if he doesn't provide any answers at least it'll put your mind at rest. Just making the effort to resolve the situation could help.' He ran his hand over my leg. 'Be positive, Ambs!'

'I guess you're right, no use fretting about it. I'll email him tomorrow to see if I can arrange another interview.'

'Attagirl! Go for it!'

The notion of seeing Professor Jonson further lightened my mood. As the two of us smoked the remainder of the cigarettes in silence, thoughts of the Professor filled my mind. I had thoroughly enjoyed the last time we'd met: I had pencilled in an hour for our interview but by the time we parted, three hours later, we had discussed more than just my research project. Much, much more. Even remembering that gave me a tinge of excitement.

Fran and I finished the final cigarette together, and all done, we sank into the swing seat cushions. We spent a while staring at the night sky: it was a clear night, the only light coming from the full moon overhead; not even the street lighting could break through the thick barrier of foliage surrounding the garden. Andrew and Nathan had long since turned out their light. Whatever they were up to, they were obviously doing it in the dark.

Francis eventually broke the silence. 'Peaceful, isn't it?'

'Beautiful, I could stay here for forever.'

'You know, none of the neighbours can see us…they can't even tell that we're here, let alone what we're doing…'

That was how Francis usually spoke when he wanted to initiate sex. We had done it in all sorts of places, even in an empty lecture theatre, just to see if we could get away with it. Which we had; the danger of being caught only made it more exciting. And being the cautious one, Francis was always the first to check that the coast was clear.

'And?' I asked, still staring at the moonlit sky, knowing full well what was on his mind.

'And?' he repeated.

I started to snigger. 'And?' I said, a little louder. A few seconds later I saw Francis' smiling face hovering over me.

'That's the first time you've laughed since—'

'So?' I smirked.

'So?' he repeated.

'I'm more relaxed now. In fact, I'm just in the right mood for—'

There was no need to finish. Francis knew exactly what I was in the mood for, and his smile became a broad grin as he knelt in front of me. Still gazing at the stars, I had to bite my lip to suppress a loud sigh as he slowly removed my underwear. We might have been alone, in the dead of night, but I still didn't want anyone to hear us. I could be quite noisy during sex, and I was finding it difficult to keep quiet as he started pleasuring me. It felt good: the first sex I'd had since the dreams began, and the first time I had felt properly positive. I was finally attempting to resolve the problem; more than that, I was going to see Professor Jonson. After the first interview, I had regretted not arranging to see him again, and now here was my chance.

I could not decide whether it was my thoughts of the Professor, Andrew's gentle massage, or Francis' delicate, turning to ferocious, stimulation, but I was responding. It was not long before my legs were instinctively tightening around Francis' head as I climaxed. Then came my stifled scream.

'Let's fuck!' I cried out, as the long-suppressed orgasm tore through me.

Francis knew his cue and lost no time in stepping out of his jogging bottoms. I helped him take hold of my oversized t-shirt and lift it over my head; I could see the eagerness in his eyes as they feasted on my nakedness. He had seen me naked loads of times before but, with our recent absence of major physical contact, this was like our first time all over again. For the past few weeks, he had been patient, respecting my reluctance, but now he was spoilt for choice, not knowing where to begin. I grabbed his hands and plastered them onto my legs, hinting at him to lift my legs around his waist. Then, our sex drought was over. Soon we were going full pelt. Not even the squeaky hinges stopped us; Francis' sharp lunges causing the seat to shake violently, back and forth. No one heard. Except Nathan, who seemed to have an ear for such things, and I could hear him shouting from the upstairs window.

'I was right! Can I join in?' came his pleading cry.

I tried to ignore him, but the more I did, the more he yelled. Eventually, my silence wore him down.

'Oh, suit yourselves, I'm going back to Andrew. At least we're having more fun up here,' Nathan sneered.

We both laughed as I waved my middle finger in his direction, deciding it would be more private if we vacated to underneath the trees: it was too early for the dew, and the long grass rubbing against our bodies only made us feel closer to nature. We must have spent at least an hour in the garden before retiring to the bedsit, where we continued until long after the sun came up.

'Thanks for seeing me at such short notice,' I said, smiling at Professor Jonson as he led me into the study of his Hammersmith flat. It was far more lavish than the bedsit in Reading, and more congenial than his office at the university where we had last met.

'It is my pleasure,' replied Jonson, in his strong Norwegian accent. 'I am sorry it has to be in the evening, I am very busy at the moment. But how could I refuse a visit from such an attractive young lady, especially one asking to see me for a second time?'

When we first met, I had noticed that Professor Jonson had an eye for the ladies. During our interview, his eyes had been scanning my body, undressing me, and his responses to my questions about his research had been saturated with innuendo. Then, when we said our goodbyes, he had forgone a formal handshake in exchange for a tight hug, followed by a lingering kiss on the cheek.

I knew a great deal of female researchers who would have reported him for his conduct, but I had rather enjoyed his flirtatious behaviour. It had been a breath of fresh air, compared to all the staid academics I had seen up until then. Indeed, he may have been some twenty years older than me, but I had still found him attractive. With thick blond hair and a lean build, he was in good shape for a forty-something. I had been itching to ask him if he worked out, but it would not have been at all professional, though afterwards I had kind of wished I had. Perhaps he had realised my attraction to him, as a psychologist he could probably read the signals I had been subconsciously providing, hence the flirting? Who knew?

'Have you had a good journey?' he enquired, pouring two glasses of sherry.

Since entering the world of senior academia, I had learnt that sherry was the staple drink of many higher-ranking academics; most PhD tutorials involved at least one glass, sometimes two.

I took a sip. 'It was okay thanks, surprisingly busy though, considering it was after rush hour.' I held the glass of sherry in front of me. 'Nice sherry this, you'll have to tell me tell the type.'

The Professor looked surprised and smiled. 'A connoisseur,' he joked. 'It is not very often we have people of your generation taking an interest in this ancient and venerable drink.' He took a sip from his own glass. 'When we have finished, I will give you a tour of my collection. If you are interested, of course?'

'That would be lovely.' I had only asked about the sherry as a way of making conversation, but after his conduct the last time we had met, and now this offer of a tour, I was beginning to suspect he had other things on his mind. He motioned me towards a large couch in the centre of the study.

'The Underground is always full of people, even at this time in the evening. I hope you did not feel uncomfortable at all? I have heard from some of my female colleagues that it can be very frightening; you never know who is about.'

'It was fine, I had no trouble.'

'I hope you will be alright going back to Reading,' he said. 'We must try to avoid finishing too late; I would hate for you to miss your last connection home.'

I smiled at his concern and held up a reassuring hand. 'No worries, Professor Jonson, I've checked the timetable and there's a late train I can catch. I've already got my return ticket, so I won't have to hang around at ticket machines or anything.'

'Very good, I am glad you have it all worked out. You would be surprised how many people come to see me and have not thought about transport home.'

I smiled and nodded, taking another sip of sherry.

'Of course, if you need to, you are more than welcome to stay here. I always have a spare room available in case of travel disruptions.'

Perhaps he did have other things on his mind, but I had promised to report back to Francis as soon as I returned home, so I had to refuse. 'Thank you, Professor, you are so kind. But I will be fine.' Though the offer did sound interesting, and the possibility that he was considering other, more intimate, things left me feeling rather flattered. But the conversation was drifting; I needed to press on. 'Now, about the reason I'm here—'

'Of course, I am sorry. Please, proceed. Tell me all about these dreams of yours.' He took a deep breath and leant forward, to emphasise his concern. 'You said they have been recurring for some time?'

For the next half an hour, we drank sherry and talked about my dream. I was impressed by his attentiveness, and his sympathy when I described the distress they were causing. He then changed the subject, asking me about my personal life and living arrangements. When I mentioned I shared a bedsit, he wanted to know about my relationship with Francis. Then he progressed onto more exacting questions: my childhood; my family; my PhD...then more intimate questions: my sexual orientation; the partners I had slept with. He assured me everything I said would remain strictly confidential, so I elected to be truthful. I wanted an answer to my dreams, and I reasoned that he would not be able to help me if I held anything back.

He had enquired about almost every aspect of my life when, out of the blue, he returned to the subject of the dream. Perhaps he had noticed my distress earlier and had changed the subject to prevent me from breaking down completely? Or, more likely, this was his method of catching me unawares so that I spoke truthfully, on his terms and at his behest. I did not care either way. I just wanted closure so I could regain some sanity, move on, and finish my PhD. He wanted to know every precise detail of the dream, which was not difficult as it was still at the forefront of my mind.

After another half an hour, we had almost finished the bottle of sherry. I could see why he had the sherry ready. It was affable, relaxing. In fact, so was the whole ambience of the room. With dimmed lighting and soft classical music, I was totally at ease and felt comfortable to speak freely. It was easy to recount the experience, and with his firm but polite interrogation I managed to recount every minute detail, even things that I had never considered before. When we finally came to the executions, the tears started, as I began to try and recreate the gory scene. The part with Zhu Fu and the Queen triggered uncontrollable sobbing, and I had to stop talking.

I felt safe and secure in his arms, as he leant across the couch to console me, and I could feel his strong muscular frame as I wrapped my arms around him. The soothing effect of the music, the sherry and the feel of his firm grip were getting to me, and I felt like the natural thing to do was to kiss him. But I knew he had to be professional, and I had to respect that.

I was impressed by his clinical attitude as he gently released me, and without hesitation continued speaking in a serious, academic tone.

'We must move forward. I will not beat around the bush as you English say. I cannot tell you the main reason for these terrible dreams, with any certainty, but I can certainly outline some possible causes. Presently, you are under a lot of stress, and when under stress the mind often behaves in strange and irregular ways. The dreams may also be your subconscious attempting to tell you something. I suggest you take a short break; step back from the causes of your stress and think about what the dream could be telling you. There is, of course, the possibility that the dream is some form of regression, or past life regression. Although many in my area of work look down on this as crank science, I do not, and I can tell you that much work has been done in this field. If you wish, I can arrange a session for proper counselling, or even hypnosis, to see if we can determine whether regression is the cause. However, what I propose you do first is opt for my earlier suggestion and think hard about the possible causes of the dream. It may be your subconscious trying to communicate a message.'

I was taken aback by his straightforward analysis. Though not definitive, it was encouraging; I just needed to look at the dream with an analytical mindset and try to figure out parallels with my own life. It was also a relief that he had not insisted on regression therapy; though the regression idea had sounded interesting I was not overly keen on the idea of hypnosis. A whole miscellany of secrets might be revealed; secrets I wanted to keep to myself.

Above all else, talking things through with him had given me confidence. Much like when I had first resolved to see the Professor in the first place.

'Thank you, Professor Jonson, you have helped me so much,' I said, bending over to hug him. The Professor started to laugh. 'What's the matter?' I asked.

'You, Amber.'

I was confused. 'Sorry?'

'After our long period of talking, you are still calling me Professor Jonson. It is Jan, Amber. Please call me Jan.'

'Oh, sorry, Professor. I mean, Jan,' I laughed.

The Professor grinned. 'That is no problem, I had only just realised.'

'How can I thank you? You have just saved my sanity! I—'

'Please, there is no need. I was glad to be of service.'

I looked at the clock and suddenly realised how late it was. I would almost certainly miss the last train home if I tried to make it to the station now. 'Damn. I've only just noticed the time. Is there any chance I could possibly take up your offer of staying the night?'

'Of course, you can stay.'

Lying in bed the next morning, in the Professor's spare room, I was in heaven. The early morning sun shone through the cracks in the curtains, and I was on the way to solving the dream. I had also spent the evening with the Professor, talking well into the night. Just lying there, I could not stop my mind from wandering. I thought of Jan's muscular frame, which I had felt when I hugged him. The thought was inviting. Relaxed and half asleep, I started imagining what might have happened if I had kissed him. After all, there was no harm indulging in a semi-conscious fantasy…

Still hugging him, I kissed him softly on the lips, running my hands over his strong back as he accepted my kiss, gripping me tighter.

'After our last meeting, I have to know, do you work out?' I asked in a hushed voice.

'Four times a week,' came his reply. 'It clears the head, makes me feel good. It's good for the mind.'

'I couldn't help noticing how fit you are.'

He smiled and kissed me even harder. Then, as he eased me back, I could see his eyes examining me.

'As your British men would say,' he whispered, 'you are quite fit yourself.'

'Thanks,' I giggled, and as I looked down with a rare shyness, I noticed the swelling in his trousers. It was irresistible. Looking him in the eye, I whispered, 'You must be feeling the same as me too,' as I rubbed my fingers against the bulge.

There was no reply; his hands gently unbuttoning my blouse told me everything I needed to know. Then, having eased the fabric apart, he started fondling my own firm abdomen.

'You work out too, yes?'

'When I can,' I murmured, enjoying his delicate caress. By now the blouse was off and his hands were tightly secured around my waist. It was obvious he was savouring what he felt. I unbuttoned and removed his shirt, he was even fitter than I had imagined, and from that moment on there was no stopping us. Our eyes were fixed on each other's bodies as I reached back and unfastened my bra, which fell freely to join the blouse on the couch. I guessed he could sense my excitement was about to explode, as the back of his hand brushed against my chest.

I was unable to keep my hands still. While I explored his firm body, he pulled me closer and we resumed our embrace. I smiled and kissed him on the lips. Then, climbing off the couch, he gazed in wonderment as I walked semi-naked towards my bag. I could feel his penetrating stare as I reached inside and pulled out a packet of condoms. His smile turned to a grin as I took one out and threw it on to the seat next to him.

He was an expert at stimulation. We both were as we played with each other. Exhausting the oral, I was ready to receive him, and he looked in anticipation as I opened the sheaf and rolled it over his hardness. It was sex, pure sex. His fitness showed, not just in his body but in his stamina, which would have put men half his age to shame. He was powerful, forceful, and all the while his eyes were fixated on me. He could not have minded me being noisy. In fact, I think he was rather chuffed with the whole experience, having sex with a girl much younger, a girl who was not afraid of taking charge, giving him much, much more than he was giving me.

We prolonged for as long as we could, the initiative ping-ponging between us: first me, then him, back to me, back to him. Next, he was leading me by the hand into his bedroom, and once on the bed I continued to work my hands over his sculptured torso. I just couldn't get enough of him.

'You are a fine, beautiful woman,' he murmured, as I lay on the bed recovering. 'And I will make proper love to you, the way you deserve.'

The lovemaking in the bedroom was the antithesis of that in the study. He was tender, considerate, and attentive, and by the morning we were both worn out.

A knock on the door brought me back to reality. The Professor was too much of a gentleman to enter a woman's bedroom without being invited. He asked if I would like tea, and after my positive response, said he would be back soon. I knew I only had minutes to end the fantasy.

He called me 'a little minx' when I suggested one final bout of passion, and he obviously could not resist, for he was pulling the bedclothes off me in readiness. 'Bout' was the best way to describe what happened next; we were fighters in the ring, competing to see who could get the most out of the session. I felt ecstatic, even confident enough to ride him bare-back; it was brilliant. But that was not enough, and he was more than willing to participate in a second, then a third round...

Then, the door opened, and in walked the Professor with a tray of tea and toast.

'Keep in touch,' Jan said, as he dropped me off at Victoria Station. 'And do not forget my suggestion:

think hard about what the dream may be telling you. Let me know how you get on.'

We shook hands, which seemed strange given what I had been imagining earlier, and after a few minutes spent waiting on the platform, I was on the train.

I had an empty carriage to myself, with just over an hour to go before we reached Reading and no distractions: it was the perfect opportunity to consider the hidden meanings of my dream. My thoughts were hazy at first; I could not help imagining my dreamt-up sex session with the Professor. But as soon as I cleared that from my mind, I could concentrate.

I thought about the Queen and her promiscuity. At first, nothing registered. Then, I thought about how many partners she had slept with: two of the King's guardsmen, the footman, and the coach driver, as well as Zhu Fu and the chambermaid…six in all. Still, nothing registered. I spent a while staring out of the window, turning it over in my mind. I decided to put myself in the Queen's place. After all, in the dream, I could feel the sword slicing through her neck.

Suddenly, the meaning started to become clear. I counted how many sexual partners I had been with over the past few months. Other than Francis, there had been five other liaisons: a lecturer, a fellow researcher, a lad from down the pub, a guy who worked in the library, and Andrew. No, six. I had forgotten Kelly. Kelly was an undergraduate at the university, who I had met several months previously. At first, it had just been occasional flirting on her part. Then she had invited me to join her friends on a night out; to cut a long story short, I had ended up sleeping at her place. We had started seeing each other, mostly in the afternoons when we should have been working on our studies. It had just been a bit of fun, until her friends grew suspicious. That was when we decided to end it.

Before the dreams, my appetite for sex had been phenomenal, and I would jump into bed with anyone, without a moment's hesitation. Perhaps the anxiety of the PhD was making me feel insecure, and the craving I had for sexual attention was my body's way of satisfying that insecurity? Come to think of it, my need for sex had also acted as a distraction from the erstwhile pressures of my research. My promiscuity certainly fit with the Queen's. But what about Francis? How did he fit into the picture?

I thought about our relationship. Was I being blind to what was really going on with Francis? Then it hit me. He was more than a friend and roommate with benefits. I should have been reading more into our friendship. He cared about me, a lot; he was always there for me, and was the one who had showed concern when I started having the dreams. I realised I cared about him too. Yes, there were others, but it was Francis who I always went back to, who I confided in. And more often than not, our sex was genuine. Not a quick session, but proper, tender, meaningful lovemaking.

Professor Jonson had been right; only I knew the answer to my dreams, I had just needed the time to figure it out. It was clear to me now, my subconscious was telling me something, warning me that my actions had consequences. If I continued the way I was going, I would lose Francis. I was the Queen, and Francis the King. If I carried on sleeping around, it would be Francis who suffered, just like the King. I was certain that Francis would not execute me, but he would almost certainly end our friendship…relationship.

Then and there, I resolved not to let Francis find out about my other flings. The only worry was Andrew. I knew he and Francis never spoke, but there was a danger that he would inadvertently let something slip, especially after one of his drunken arguments with Nathan. Deciding to meet with Andrew and end our relationship as soon as I got back, I relaxed into my seat with the calm satisfaction of achieving closure.

It was mid-afternoon and Francis was out when I arrived back at the bedsit. Next to his bed were two glasses and an empty wine bottle. I frantically started scanning my memory, trying to figure out who had been here. It could not have been one of his mates, else there would have been beer cans lying about. So, it must have been a woman.

My suspicions were confirmed when I started making his bed and smelt perfume. I decided to wash the sheets, there was no way I was going to sleep in that room with the smell of someone else's perfume still lingering about. The local laundrette was only down the road, so I took them there and grabbed myself a coffee from across the road, sipping it slowly and dragging on several cigarettes while I waited for the laundry to finish.

Professor Jonson had treated me to lunch at an expensive restaurant in Victoria before I left, so I was not especially hungry. Really, it should have been me treating him, to thank him for setting me on the right path. But he insisted on paying which had only added to my jubilation. The nightmare dreams had almost been sorted, and my fantasy dream of great sex, loads of great sex, had still been on my mind. I smiled. Professor Jonson was a sweet and thoughtful man, I was fortunate to know him.

'You're back then,' were the first words Francis said to me, when he walked through the door later that afternoon. I had just finished putting fresh sheets on the bed and was calming my nerves with yet another cigarette. I was not looking forward to the talk we were about to have.

'You too,' I said, before taking a long drag on my cigarette, filling the room with a cloud of expelled smoke. I wanted to get in first. 'I see you had company last night,' I nodded towards the empty bottle and glasses.

'I did,' was his reply. 'Had a good night yourself?'

'Yes, thanks.' The atmosphere was strained.

'How was Professor Jonson?'

'He was alright.' I knew this conversation was going to be difficult.

Francis came straight out with it. 'You were shagging him, weren't you?'

'No. We had a good long chat, and he sorted my dreams out. We just talked.'

'Don't lie, Ambs, you were shagging him, weren't you?'

I knew I had to stand my ground. Nothing had happened, though considering what I had been fantasising it was difficult to come across as honest.

'We had a long talk, and it was late, so he let me stay in his spare room.'

'Yeah, like that's what really happened. I knew you fancied him. After the first interview all you did was talk about how brilliant he was.'

'He's a great guy, Fran, I admit that. But there was no sex last night. I swear to you. What about you, anyway. Who were you shagging last night? Some slut I guess, from the smell of the perfume she left behind.'

Francis was silent for a moment. Then he looked me dead in the eye and said, in an emotionless voice, 'Jane Smith'.

Given what I had previously been up to, I couldn't argue much. But that name infuriated me. 'Jane Smith! Busty Jane from Letters, the faculty bike! She's shagged everyone, Fran.'

'Yes, well.'

'How did Jane Smith manage to get into your bed?'

'She phoned and said she was having trouble with a paper she was working on, so I said she could come round. I knew you'd be back, so I wasn't planning—'

I finished his sentence. 'But I didn't come back, so you—'

He continued. 'We opened a bottle of wine and—'

'One thing led to another, and you ended up shagging.'

'That's about it. What about you?'

By then, I had calmed down. There was no use arguing, and I had to forgive him, especially with my history. 'I got quite emotional recounting all the details of the dream, then he started asking such personal questions, and I just broke down.'

'He put his arms around you and—'

'Yep, you've got it. But it was just a hug.'

'That's roughly how it happened with Jane, except we—'

'Except it wasn't her dream, it was her research, or so she claimed,' I said, shaking my head in disappointment.

'Or so she claimed. I don't know.'

'Look, why don't we just call it quits?'

Francis agreed. 'It's quits,' he said, putting his arm around me.

I think he was relieved we had resolved the matter, and I was thankful we had put it behind us, so we could move on to the conversation I had planned. I told him how the Professor had encouraged me to explore what the dreams might be telling me. Even threw in the possibility of regression for good measure, though I left out my conclusion that they were warning me of my promiscuous behaviour. I had to be careful or else chances of reconciliation would have been nil. Instead,

I put the dreams down to all the stress I was under and having so many things going on.

'Essentially, I'm frightened of losing you,' I said, relived when he instantly replied.

'Me too. Look, how about we put aside the past, and start with a new beginning. Be an exclusive couple.'

'Exclusive?' I repeated, surprised. 'Just us? Sounds good to me!'

He repeated 'just us', smiling, though his emphasis on the word 'just' told me he must have had his suspicions. Oh well, I wasn't going to push it. The important thing was that our future together was about to begin.

Though we could barely afford it, we celebrated with a meal, drinks, and his freshly made bed, where we continued to enjoy each other's company for the rest of the evening.

The next day, I made a point of forgetting all about the others, a job made easier by the fact they were nearly all in the past, and most had gone to pastures new. The hardest was going to be Andrew. I knew from our trysts that he usually returned from his nightshift around eight and had the flat to himself while Nathan was at work. But, when I went upstairs to see him, I found their room empty. Apparently, the night I was with Professor

Jonson, Nathan had caught Andrew in a passionate clinch with the DJ. According to the neighbour who told me, when they came back there was the usual banging of doors and crashing of furniture. Of course, Nathan's screaming woke everyone, except Francis, who was too preoccupied with 'Busty Jane' to notice, otherwise he would have been only too pleased to tell me the gays had left. The last the neighbour saw of Andrew, he was getting into a battered old Transit van with 'Hot Stuff Disco' emblazoned across the side, being driven by an attractive female.

As for Francis, for almost the next twelve months we stayed together, this time as a proper couple. Then Francis was offered a lecturing job in Manchester and agreed that, while we had enjoyed our time together, it was time we moved on.

I stayed in contact with Professor Jonson. He was pleased Francis and I had got together and was equally pleased when we eventually parted on good terms. It was just after Francis had left that Jan suggested I give up the bedsit and move in with him. At the time, his idea seemed logical: my university allowance had gone, and the small pieces of research work I was getting would never have paid the rent, let alone food and essentials. It would also give me time to find a more permanent place, after finding a full-time position of course. We decided we could never be in a proper relationship. Besides the age difference, we knew the nature of our work meant one or both of us would almost certainly have to move to another part of the country sometime.

Eighteen months we stayed together, until one day he announced he was retiring and going to live with his daughter in Canada. At first, I was devastated. Despite securing a regular a lecturing job, there was no way I could afford a place of my own, not at London prices. The Professor had helped me to write a couple of papers based on my work, and I had just started writing a book, but that was not going to bring in much money.

I need not have worried. Jan had decided to keep the flat as a London base, if and when he needed to return to England for business or pleasure, and he was very happy for me to live there as long as I wanted. He never did return, but we remained in contact for a while, until, other than the occasional Christmas or birthday card, our correspondence dried up. I will always remember Professor Jonson. It was he who encouraged me to take my work further; with several highly cited papers to my name, an acclaimed book published, and a top teaching post, I have become a renowned expert in my field.

I still live in Professor Jonson's flat, which I now share with my new partner. As for the dream, I have recently made some startling discoveries. Professor Jonson was always interested in the possibility of mind regression, and though I shied away from his suggested hypnosis, I did follow through with a less intrusive idea of his. Once I had become an established lecturer, I set my students a project to determine whether there was any truth behind the story of the royal birth. I tasked one group with researching international folklore, and another group with investigating my family tree.

The first group came back with an obscure Turkish folktale, about a King whose Queen had been executed for her impropriety. The story went that the non-royal baby which she gave birth to was given for adoption in another country. There the story dried up, until the second group traced my family back several generations, to discover that one of my relatives, a baby girl, had been handed anonymously to a group of Catholic nuns, who in turn had passed her up for adoption to a Cypriot family. Of course, whether these findings have any bearing on the story in my dream is still open to debate. But not for me.

A few weeks ago, I took a DNA test. As my mother was Cypriot and my father was English, I was not surprised when this was reflected in my DNA. What did surprise me were the traces of Chinese heritage, which no one could explain, except perhaps me, and Professor Jan Jonson.

Watched

Seventeen floors up. She is one of those who rarely closes the curtains. After all, no one can see in. Except for him, on the seventeenth floor of the block opposite. At first, he thought there would be no use for the telescope the kids brought him for Christmas.

'To look at the stars at night,' they had said. 'You're always going on about space, rockets, and all that.'

He did try at first, but it was no good. Too much light pollution from the city lights. Instead, he found himself looking at the streets around him, which turned out to be much more interesting. One time he had witnessed a mugging. He would have called the police, but he had not been able to remember the name of the street where it happened. Would they even have listened? A bumbling old man calling in, with a vague report of someone being mugged? What would they think of him watching the streets through his telescope, anyway? They probably would have accused him of stalking. Too many questions might have been asked; it had been best to leave things as they were.

Saturday is the night she always goes out, but it is still early enough for a sneak peek. There she is, just entered the room. She has already changed out of her work uniform and into the long t-shirt she usually wears around the flat. Oh, now it's time to change again. What will it be tonight? Usually it's a nice black number. Not too revealing, but still enough for her to be attractive. Week in, week out, she returns with some man or other. Usually, it's a different one each week. Some stay the night and leave the next morning; others leave as soon as they are done.

Wow, no black tonight, she's wearing a new red dress! Out to impress. She must be after someone special this week. A couple of weeks ago she brought back a lad. Much too young for her, but it was brilliant watching their performance: in the kitchen, the lounge, and then in the bedroom. He didn't blame her, the lad had been cute, and they had been a pleasure to watch.

His thoughts are on the red dress, with little else underneath, as he watches her switch off the light and leave the flat. Who is she after? No need to dwell on it, he will find out soon enough. Dozing off in front of the television, he wakes to find the light is on opposite. Going as fast his old legs will take him, he hobbles over to the telescope. Eh, another girl? So, this must be who she was out to impress. Tonight should be interesting, he has never watched two women before.

The following Saturday and she is in the red dress again. He hopes she will come back with same girl, so he can enjoy a repeat of their last, epic performance. But she will not be back for a while, if she comes back at all this time, so he will have to occupy himself in the meantime. He is fed up of watching TV. That lad she had the other week was nice…it had been a long time since he himself had indulged. Taking his book of numbers from the sideboard, he flicks through. None of the contacts were cute enough, nowhere near as cute as the lad. He continues flicking. Jonathan. Ah, now he was cute. A bit short notice, but he might be free.

Call made. Jonathan arrives. Charges him double: it is a Saturday night after all, and very short notice. Worth it though. Three hours of pure heaven. Then, time to go; he pays Jonathan and promises to call him soon. They kiss in the hallway on the way out; Jonathan says he is the best he's had all week, though he probably says that to everyone, especially the gullible good payers. A little extra cash to see Jonathan over the weekend, another kiss, and he's all alone again.

Half asleep in his chair, he catches sight of a light coming on across the street. She's home. Who is it this time? Could be that cute lad again, that would be nice, the perfect way to round off an evening spent with Jonathan. But no, it's the other girl. He is fascinated by how quickly a bottle of wine is opened, and drunk. Then, straight to the bedroom. Again, he is mesmerised by the sight of the two women. He has seen two men loads of times, even his own performance, when a friend made a video of him with some other bloke. Never knew his name, he never thought to ask. In any case, if he was a professional, he would have given a false name, they all did. Anonymity was the name of the game, or so his friend said. Still, the money came in handy, especially with the kid's birthdays coming up.

It had been a long day and he wants to go to bed, except he is frightened of missing something. He eventually falls asleep in the armchair next to the telescope. It is daylight when he wakes; he has probably missed a good part of the action. He looks through the telescope. They are in the kitchen. The other girl must have stayed the night again. Good, there might be another session to watch, round two.

He was right. They finish breakfast and start again, their lovemaking more intense than it has ever been before. Most of the day his eye is glued to the telescope; getting food to eat is a problem and going to the toilet is an occupational hazard. Just past teatime and the other girl leaves. Show over.

Much of the following week is the same as usual. She gets up, dresses into her uniform for work, then comes home, changes, and spends the rest of the evening lounging about the flat. Her normal routine, though this week she is spending more time on the phone. Perhaps it's her new girlfriend she's talking to. Saturday comes around and there is a repeat of the previous few weekends. She goes off out; Jonathan comes round; she returns with the other girl. It is the same the following Saturday, and the one after that, and the one after that. The truth is, it's wearing him out; not just physically, but his finances too. Jonathan's good, with an athletic physique and great stamina, but he is charging more and more each week. Says he is his special customer and must turn other work down to accommodate him.

He decides to give Jonathan a rest one Saturday; just as well really, for that night she returns early, with an extra treat in store. Not just the girl but the cute lad as well. Watching the three of them is bliss. He makes sure he stays awake so he can watch the whole show, and none of them are failing to please.

It's just before nine a.m. and he is busy watching the activity opposite. Nothing special: the three of them are having breakfast. Still worth a peek though, if only to admire the beauty of their youth. He is just beginning to wonder about their conversation when there is a sudden knock at the door. Other than his family, and Jonathan, he rarely has visitors, and if he did, they would have to first ring the downstairs buzzer. So, who could it be? He freezes in a cold sweat: the police? Someone has reported him? In an instant he pictures the court case; the newspaper stories: 'elderly pervert stalking young girl in flat opposite'.

All the fun and excitement of the past few hours, days, weeks, months swiftly dissipate as he tries to prepare for what is to come. There is a second, louder knock. He had better go, else they might start battering the door down. He imagines the police barging in, shouting their instructions for him to remain still. Get rid of the evidence, yes, that's it. With no evidence, they won't have a case. Hide the telescope. Bury it in the wardrobe, under some clothes; if they find it he can tell them it was given to him for Christmas, but he's never used it, too much street lighting and all that. At least that would be somewhere near the truth. But the family's seen it, even Jonathan's seen it…in their enquiries the police were bound to interview them. A third knock. He is dripping with panicked sweat. He had to answer, there was no other option.

Hesitantly opening the door, he is overwhelmed with relief when he sees Jonathan. He gives him a huge hug.

'My, someone's pleased to see me,' says a surprised Jonathan.

'You wouldn't believe how pleased I am to see you,' replies the watcher. 'Come on in, this is a nice surprise, what can I do for you? It's a bit early for a session, and I must admit, I can't really afford to pay much right now.'

'Ah, no worries,' laughs Jonathan. 'In fact, I think you're due for a freebie.'

The watcher's face lights up, already more than pleased that it is not the police. 'Really, that would be nice.'

'I'm sure I've got time for a quickie,' winks Jonathan.

'Is that really why you're here?'

'No, not really ...'

'Well, why are you here then?'

'A friend asked me to give you this,' says Jonathan holding out an envelope.

'What is it?'

'You'll see. But you're not to open it until after I've gone.'

'Right. Well, would you like a cup of tea while you're here? I've just boiled the kettle.'

'No thanks, I've got someone waiting.'

'My, you're popular.'

'I'm too good,' smiles Jonathan. 'But I must go, give me a call when you need me next. Remember it's a freebie.'

They say their goodbyes and the watcher is sitting at the breakfast table, staring at the envelope. He wonders what it could be. The suspense is simply too great to bear, and he tears it open. Inside is a DVD, with a message written in thick black marker pen. 'Especially for you,' it says, accompanied by a kiss made with fresh lipstick. Intrigued, he rushes into the front room where he puts the disc into the DVD player and switches on the television. A familiar face appears on the screen, the girl from the flat opposite. She is wearing the now familiar red dress.

'Hope you've been enjoying the show,' she says, blowing a kiss. 'Because I have too, and I've got a little something special for you. Just for you.'

The screen fades to his block of flats, and he is dumbstruck as the camera zooms in on his window. For the next few minutes, he is watching himself: getting undressed; getting dressed; having a meal; watching television; then him with Jonathan. In shock, he looks out of the window to the girl's flat. His eyesight is too poor to get a clear view, so he goes to telescope. He sees the girl and her friend, arm in arm, and Jonathan with the cute lad, arm in arm as well. The two couples are smiling, then laughing, eagerly waving in his direction.

Amanda

Amanda: the immaculately dressed brunette sitting at the head of the table. My ex, though we are still friends, good friends; it was her who landed me this job in the first place. She has come a long way since we first met. Back then she had been doing bits of secretarial and admin work; filling supermarket shelves; even flipping burgers at McDonalds. It had been a hard life, but she had been content. Then, she had landed a job as Rupert's PA. Rupert is the company chairman, silver haired but not unattractive, currently sitting next to her. You see, Amanda's clever, and cunning enough to see an opportunity when it arises. Once she landed the job it was not long before she was helping Rupert run his business, and despite being some twenty-five years his junior, not long before they were married.

Sucked into the world of tough financial management, she soon adopted Rupert's ruthless business attitude. Now she is someone to fear, except for me. I know Amanda better than anyone else. I have not told anyone else in the company this, but I can say with complete certainty that working for, and marrying, Rupert was part of an agenda. It was all for the wealth and luxury, not love or anything sentimental like that. Though in part, the same could be said of Rupert. Besides her tenacity and organised mind, Amanda was a dangerous bit of rough, who brought fun and adventure to his erstwhile, boring existence.

However, whilst Amanda's days of partying are now over, like her penchant for tattoos and piercings (all now carefully concealed), some things haven't changed. She might appear to be the perfect suburban housewife; a successful business partner; someone who lives the high-society life of foreign holidays, clean eating and fitness training in her own personal gym, which she had Rupert build for her. But deep down, she is still the mischievous, reckless Amanda of old.

The rumours are that Rupert's looking for a new, younger model. Fiona Lancaster, Rupert's new PA, is the name regularly mentioned by the office gossips. Nothing can be proven, of course, but she has been spending a lot of time in Rupert's office lately, and recently accompanied him on a business trip to New

York, alone. The same rumours suggest that Amanda has figured this out and is having an affair with one of the new trainees, just to spite her husband. Many think it's all just office tittle-tattle, but as I have said, I know Amanda better than most. Under that hard, ruthless exterior, she is still the licentious, flirtatious Amanda she has always been. No one seems to have noticed that her recent intake of trainees has been made up almost entirely of young, fit stallions; I would not be surprised if she hasn't already had several secret affairs, as retribution against Rupert, or just for fun. The rumour concerning Rupert looking for someone new may also have some truth to it, since Amanda was once his 'younger model', as was Rupert's previous wife, Clare.

So here we are, Friday afternoon, stuck in a meeting which has been underway for just over forty minutes. Each year we go through this same ritual: discussing the company's annual report prior to publication. It would make much more sense to give each of us a copy of the report to look through. That way, if there was anything that needed to be changed, we could simply pass on our comments. Still, having a big, group discussion about it did while away an afternoon, and saved us all from working on the last day before the long Easter weekend. Plus, there was the added bonus of Amanda chairing the meeting, which worked wonders at taking away the boredom. I gaze at her, drooling over her amiable appearance, something for my vivid imagination to fantasise over.

As is usual at these meetings, everyone is going through the motions of smiling, laughing and feigning interest; whatever is necessary to win brownie points. Our finance director, the suave Jonny Smyth, one of Amanda's earliest appointments, has just started his ramble about the company's annual results. This was going to be heavy going. I look across to Amanda and her eyes are fixed on Jonny and his flipchart. I wonder what is going through her mind. Whatever it is, I can guarantee that she is only going through the motions, pretending to look interested.

Watching her eyes, I can tell that she is mentally undressing Jonny, imagining having her wicked way with him. Amanda always got what she wanted in the end, so good news for Jonny, lucky bugger. Yes, Jonny was married, but that had never stopped Amanda in the past. Whatever! She could fantasise about whatever she wanted. I knew what I was visualising: the exquisiteness of Amanda's new form, and how different our lovemaking would be if we were still together.

A hot summer's day and Amanda summons me over to see her. She sounds agitated on the phone.

'I'll tell you when you get here,' she snaps.

Passing through the massive gates guarding her marital mansion, I see the BMW parked on the gravel drive, the BMW Rupert bought her for her birthday. Approaching the front door, I shelter under the porch from the mid-day sun and ring the doorbell, waving up to the surveillance camera to let her know it's me at the door. No answer. I ring again and wait. Ring a third time. Still no answer. Perhaps she had to go out, except…her car is on the drive…she never goes anywhere without her pride and joy. I ring a fourth time and continue to wait, still no response. Maybe she had to go out with Rupert, his Mercedes is not there. Or perhaps she is in the garden, she loves her sunbathing…but the bell has an extension, so she would have heard it. And she is expecting me.

I am about to give up and leave, when a white shape comes hurrying towards the door. It reaches the door and an icy blast from the air conditioning hits me as the door opens. From the dampness of her bath robe, it is clear that she has just got out of the shower. Thoughts of her nakedness beneath the robe excite me, as she pulls me inside and the door slams shut. Before I can even say hello, I am pinned against the wall, a pair of lips being forced against mine.

The room bursts into laughter. I have missed the joke, but laugh anyway, I must at least appear to be concentrating. It seems the joke was at the expense of Stuart, the latest of Amanda's stallions. His face is reddening. Glancing in Amanda's direction, I see her smiling at Stuart. I have seen that expression before, too many times. Now I know who the subject of her affection is. I look towards Stuart again. Yes, there it is, a slight smile in Amanda's direction. The interaction between the two is unmistakable.

Stuart is still blushing and is trying his hardest not to be seen looking in Amanda's direction. Amanda sees my stare and I am sure I see a quick wink in my direction before her gaze returns to Stuart. The joke subsides and Jonny resumes his oration. Normality is restored.

No time to talk, let alone think, as I am dragged up the polished wooden staircase, into the main bedroom, and onto the fine cotton sheets of a king-sized bed. Amanda's hands are unceremoniously tearing my clothes off, throwing them down to join her robe, which is already on the floor. Her assertiveness is overpowering, the sex rudimentary.

'What's going on?' I ask, as she lifts her robe up off the floor.

'Tell you in a minute,' comes her reply, as she walks out of the room.

On returning, she hands me a similar robe which I assume to be Rupert's. I move to sit alongside her on the bed. 'What's going on?' I ask again.

Lifting an ashtray from the bedside cabinet and placing it on her lap, she insists on having a cigarette before answering any questions. Her anxiety shows. She stopped smoking years ago, and her hand trembles as she lights the final cigarette in the packet. Flicking the ash into the overflowing ashtray, she passes me the cigarette. I take a drag, before passing it back to her. We continue until the cigarette is finished.

I suddenly notice the clock on my side of the bed. 'Christ, is that the time!' I exclaim. 'What time is Rupert home?'

Amanda leans over and deliberately stares at the clock. A long dramatic pause. 'Never,' is all she says.

Still frightened about us being caught, it takes a few moments for me to realise what she has said. I ask again what is going on.

'Never,' repeats Amanda, before going on to explain that Rupert has left her and wants a divorce.

There is a collective sigh as Jonny finishes and sits down.

'Thank you, Johnny,' says Amanda with a smile, trying her hardest not to show how relived she is that he has finished. 'Now, Rupert will grace us with his Chairman's report, which I believe is as positive as Jonny's financial report.'

A silent yawn ripples around the table as Rupert stands. Normally it is the polished report from the annual accounts he reads out; this year will probably be no different, page after page of pure bull. Oh well, at least it gives me more time to think about Amanda.

'Thank you, Amanda,' begins Rupert.

But what is this? Stuart is sitting up and straightening awkwardly. His body language is showing discomfort, and Amanda is trying to signal at him to calm down. Hmmm…interesting.

Entering Amanda's kitchen, I find Stuart sitting at the table, drinking coffee. His face drops when he sees me. Amanda, who is preparing breakfast, glances across, gasps, and pulls together the over-sized corduroy shirt she is wearing. She looks at Stuart, then back to me.

'Morning,' she says, with a forced smile. She turns to me. 'Stuart occasionally comes to sort the garden out.' Then to Stuart. 'Peter sometimes stays over when he is working late with me and Rupert.'

I have an uneasy feeling that I am being looked at. I momentarily glance over to Amanda and almost immediately she averts her eyes from me, looking back at Stuart. Rupert is rambling on, but while trying to listen, I cannot help noticing the way Stuart reacts to Amanda. Then, a realisation. Fiona is seated next to Amanda and based on her occasional uneasiness it is possible that she thinks she herself is the object of Stuarts gaze. She is mistaken though; Stuart is definitely making eye contact with Amanda. It appears none of the others have noticed the action going on between Amanda and Stuart; everyone is either doodling on their pads or concentrating on Rupert. But someone will eventually notice, and put two and two together; then, they'll tell all their friends about it, and the rumour concerning Amanda's affair will gain traction. In the meantime, Rupert still rattles on.

Stuart straightens as he sits up; the tight t-shirt he is wearing revealing his fitness. It's a distraction from the disarray the table is in, with the tablecloth half hanging off and an overturned vase, leaking water…something has happened, something violent…perhaps something passionate.

'Hello, Stuart,' I say, holding out my hand, whilst simultaneously noticing that the chairs have been pushed aside. Stuart nervously holds out his hand to meet mine. His grip is strong.

'Hello,' is his only reply, as we shake hands.

Amanda points to coffee machine. 'Help yourself, I'll be with you in a minute.'

I pour a coffee and sit opposite Stuart, who keeps glancing across at Amanda. I continue to make conversation. Small talk, centring on gardening, work, and the warm weather. But, while we are talking, I cannot help admiring the exquisiteness of his build. And all the while, Amanda keeps glancing across.

'Sorry, I must go, Mrs Hobbs. I've a couple of big jobs this morning,' Stuart says, as he rises from his chair. 'Thanks for letting me have the money, it will be a great help.'

'My pleasure,' replies Amanda, with an air of relief. She gives Stuart a hug. 'Wish Chloe a happy birthday from me, you must bring her round sometime, I'd love to meet her. Perhaps one evening, for dinner or something.'

'I will, that would be great,' says Stuart. 'Chloe always says that she would love to live in a house like this, so she would definitely say yes to—'

Amanda stops him with a light kiss on the lips, and from the renewed reddening of his face, I can tell there is something I am not privy to.

'Well, make sure to bring her round then. That's an order!' she says, her face hardening with mock severity.

Stuart relaxes and laughs. 'Yes, miss, whatever you say, miss.'

Amanda cheerily shakes his hand. 'Get on with you. I'll see you at work Monday, and as usual next week. Don't forget that the trees need trimming.'

'Okay, I'll see to it. Bye, Mrs Hobbs.' He turns awkwardly to me. 'Bye—'

'Goodbye, Stuart,' I reply, cutting him short.

Amanda is smiling as we both watch Stuart leave the kitchen. A few seconds later, we hear the slam of the front door. Amanda returns to the work surface next to the window. She is too engrossed in preparing breakfast to notice me approaching from behind. Joining her, I can feel the slenderness of her waist as I rest my hands on her corduroy shirt.

Gently pressing my lips against her neck, I murmur into her ear, 'Morning, how did you sleep?'

'Morning, babes. Good thanks, how are you this morning?' she replies softly.

'Top of the world,' I answer, as I pull her around to face me. 'More importantly, how are you?'

She kisses me on the lips. 'So much better than yesterday. Thanks for last night, and definitely thanks for yesterday afternoon. The sex was brilliant!'

'It's the least I could do,' I smile. Then, changing the subject, 'Nice lad, Stuart.'

'It's his girlfriend's birthday on Wednesday, so he came round to ask if I could pay him a week early. Apparently, he is planning something special for her. He is cute, though, isn't he? I could see you ogling him earlier.'

'You can say that again.'

'So, you—'

I look in Amanda's direction; again, she is meeting my stare. No averting her eyes this time. I smile and she smiles back. I discretely nod in Stuart's direction and her smile turns to grin. I grin back, but as I do, she holds her finger to her lips. It's a secret she wants kept. She looks around to see if anyone else is watching, then points to Rupert, who is repeating the same sales figures that Jonny has already covered. I wink at her then look back at Rupert, pretending to listen. But I keep thinking about Stuart and Amanda, out of envy or curiosity, I cannot decide which. Bordering on the side of envy, I start to conjure scenarios of them together.

Amanda is sunbathing in an isolated corner of the garden, and Stuart is trimming an adjacent tree. The sun is beating down, and he has taken his top off; he knows Amanda is watching and deliberately takes his time, provocatively stretching, reaching out, then bending. Making sure Amanda gets the best view of his superbly sculpted torso. All the while, there is flirtatious eye contact. Amanda waves him over to join her with a bottle of wine. Their conversation is full of playful innuendo. Then Amanda dives in and asks about his relationship with Chloe. At first bashful, Stuart is shy of revealing too much. Then, as the wine takes effect, he reveals his anxieties about Chloe and her apparent sexual prowess. Amanda smiles impishly, the conversation continues, becoming increasingly deep, increasing sexual, until…they are naked on the grass.

'Sorry, Rupert. Paul, have you any views on this,' asks Amanda sharply, dragging me back to reality.

I see Amanda glaring at Paul from Sales. It seems his concentration, too, was wandering, and I am thankful Amanda did not single me out as an example to everyone. Paul tries muddling through some form of answer before Amanda interrupts him.

'Pay attention next time,' she snaps, inviting Rupert to continue. She looks at me and winks. She must know I am not concentrating either...perhaps, the wink was a sign that she had deliberately chosen not to pick on me...perhaps, I am one of her favourites. We do have a history after all.

On one of the sun loungers, next to the pool, Amanda is lifting a magnum of Champagne out of a silver ice bucket.

'Another glass?' she asks, wiping away the excess moisture. As she pours, she comments on how she and Rupert were saving it for their wedding anniversary. Then, nodding towards the ice bucket, on how it was a wedding present from the office. 'They said we were such a great team, that we would always be celebrating,' she laughs. 'Bet they never thought I would be celebrating like this though.'

'It's the two of us who are celebrating now,' I reply, clinking my glass against hers.

'To us,' agrees Amanda. 'It's our celebration now, back together.'

'To the future,' I continue, lifting my glass in salute.

'The future' she repeats, taking a sip.

I yawn and look around the table. Following the incident involving Paul, everyone is now listening diligently. Amanda is policing the table while Rupert continues. Her glower is enough to make anyone sit up and take notice, except for me, who she keeps smiling at.

The champagne is finished, and we are lying there, enjoying the sun. After a while, Amanda seems to grow restless.

Out the blue, she suddenly shouts, 'Race you three times around the pool. The winner decides what we do next!'

The second lap and we are level pegging, though being fitter, it looks like an easy win for Amanda. The start of the third lap and she is well ahead, but I muster a quick spurt of energy, and as we approach the diving board, the agreed finish line, we are side by side again. A nudge of my elbow into Amanda's side.

'Bastard!' she shrieks, as she hits the water, splashing her arms to stay afloat. She eventually manages to put her feet on to the bottom. 'That's cheating,' she gasps, catching her breath. 'Well, I suppose you had better come in and claim your prize.'

Diving in, it is only seconds before I reach her.

'Okay, your decision. What do you want to do?' she asks, smiling.

Leaning forward, I whisper in her ear. She steps back in feigned shock—

Rupert raises his voice as he mentions Fiona. Everyone looks in her direction. There is discomfort in her posture as she tries to cope with the attention. No one else, except me, can see Amanda's surprise. Rupert is congratulating Fiona on completing a special project he had set her, and everyone's imagination must be running wild as he goes on to say how good she was.

The kitchen blinds are open. 'Hadn't we better close the blinds?' I ask, sliding open Amanda's unbuttoned corduroy shirt. 'The neighbours might see and take tales back to Rupert.'

'We are secluded enough here,' Amanda replies, nodding to the window behind her. 'The house is surrounded by so many walls and trees, no one will see in. Anyway, it's all part of the adventure, isn't it?' Then, frustrated with the unnecessary interruption, she wraps her hands around my neck. 'So, just get on with it.'

I can feel her naked legs tight around my hips, and the table creaks as our sex becomes frantic. The phone rings.

'Don't stop, it'll go to voice mail!' Amanda screams. Five more rings, then it stops. 'Bastard probably had the wrong number,' she murmurs.

The phone rings again. We wait. Six rings and the answer phone kicks in. The recording starts. Amanda's legs release me as she remains relaxed, resting on to her elbows. She raises her middle finger towards the phone as Rupert's voice comes over speaker.

'Hello, Amanda, it's me,' the voice says.

'Cunt,' she mouths as I step back to listen. 'Trust the bastard to ring now. I bet he's wired up a camera so he can watch us.'

Rupert continues with his message. 'I've been thinking, you can keep the flat in Archway, I'll have the house. I deem that fair compensation for what you are going through, and it would save us a lot of trouble. I am sure you will accept that? I've been onto my solicitors; I'm admitting all blame so there will be no problems for you, in fact, you'll probably come out of this better than I will. Over the next couple of days, you should get the divorce papers to sign. But I think it would be best if you did not contact me. If you want to speak, do it through my solicitors, alright? And stay away from Fiona. I know you are angry, and you have every right to be, but she does not deserve to be spoken to like you spoke to her yesterday.' Rupert pauses for a moment. 'I think that's about it. Oh, as to moving out, contact my solicitors and they will arrange any help you need.'

The message ends, and Amanda looks to me.

'It's finished then. Five years of marriage and not even a goodbye! But at least he has admitted fault.' There is jubilation in her voice as she continues. 'I've won! I've got the flat!' She reaches up and high-five's me.

I grin as I look at Fiona, Amanda, and Rupert in rotation, imagining how Amanda could have upset Fiona.

'Mr Hobbs' office, Fiona speaking. How can I help you?'

'Can you put Rupert on, please?'

'Oh, is that you Mrs Hobbs? I'm afraid he's in a meeting.'

'I want to speak to him—'

'He's really tied up at moment, but I'll ask him to call as soon as he's free. Can I take a message?'

'Look, bitch, put the bastard on now! I know he's there. He always tells you to say he's in a meeting when he doesn't want to speak to someone, doesn't he? Fucking meeting! Remember, I did your fucking job once.'

'Don't you dare speak to Fiona like that,' Rupert cuts in on another line. 'What do you want?'

'What's all this about a divorce, couldn't you have told me last night?

'Like I said in the message, we are not getting on and now we're drifting apart—'

As Amanda continues, there's the sound of Fiona sobbing on the first line. 'I suppose you'll be shacking up with your new bit of stuff, then?' Fiona's sobbing gets louder. 'What's your excuse? She's got better tits than me, is that it?

'Actually, they're quite—'

'Bet she's not as good as me, though—'

'She's actually quite—' Rupert breaks off, as he realises what he's just said.

'So, you have been screwing her then!' screams Amanda. Then louder, to make sure Fiona can hear on the other line, 'You must be after his fucking money darling, because you must have realised by now what a crap screw he is!'

Rupert is still wittering on. I have no idea what he's on about, I lost the thread ages ago. Amanda smiles in my direction again. Can she read my mind? Probably not, but I am sure she's thinking about me. Secretly lusting after me, like I'm lusting after her. I think of what Amanda said about Rupert, not long after they got married. Regimented and mechanical was how she described their sex, before going on to say how she longed for our spontaneity and adventure. Our spontaneity and adventure.

We are discussing our future plans over dinner.

'No need to worry about money, the flat is all paid for, and the income from the divorce will be more than enough to cover household bills,' Amanda says with a grin. 'We will never need to work again, babes.'

I respond, with a half-smile, 'Yes, but I don't want to give up work, not just yet. Besides, I enjoy the job.'

'Of course, I understand. I was just saying. Your salary can provide some pocket money; that little bit extra to enjoy ourselves with.'

The room bursts into applause. Rupert has finally finished, and adopts his usual, self-satisfied smile. He is lapping up the attention, and I am sure I catch him looking in Fiona's direction. Then, the mantle falls to one of Rupert's appointments, our Sales Director, Candice, or 'sexy Candy' as some of guys refer to her. She's another one who always gives a marathon spiel.

Amanda is not paying attention, too busy sharing a secret smile with Stuart. Neither notice my gaze, as I flick between them. Envy becomes jealousy. Amanda and Stuart? Together? No! Amanda is mine!

Another warm summer's day, and I am walking along Archway; Amanda's BMW is parked outside the flat. On entering, I hear a dull thud coming from the bedroom, and swiftly go to investigate. Carefully edging the bedroom door open, I see clothes scattered all over the floor; the sound must have been a trainer hitting the uncarpeted wooden floor. I open the door a little further, just enough to see what is going on in the room, and discover Amanda, sitting astride Stuart.

Stuart is in the raw, he is the Adonis I imagined, and against Amanda's superb flawlessness…I am lost in staring. Then, anger takes hold. She is mine, not Stuart's. I must make a move; put a stop to this. Pulling out my mobile, I select and call her number. Hearing it ring in the bedroom, I glance around the door to see her reaching for her jeans, which are conveniently sprawled nearby.

'Hello, where are you?' she asks, seeing my name on the display.

I lie. 'I'm tied up at work, where are you?'

She lies too. 'I'm in the British Library, getting some figures for next week's presentation. Can't talk too long, the security man heard the phone and he's giving me a dirty look.'

Interesting research this, and funny security man, I think, as I watch her stroke Stuarts chest whilst he plays with her hair.

'Look, umm, I was hoping to see you. We need to talk.'

'What's up?'

I go straight to the point. 'Are you seeing Stuart?'

'Oh, Stuart?' Stuart, who is now tickling Amanda. She tries to stop him, and Stuart goes to speak but she silently shushes him just in time, mouthing my name in his direction.

'Yes, Stuart.'

'No, of course not,' she says. 'Whatever makes you think that?

'I don't know. It's just a feeling. He's always around; always at the house.' I anticipate a quick reply, denying everything, but all I hear is silence. I glance through the crack in the door again. She is trying her hardest not to giggle as Stuart starts tickling her again. The next sound over the phone is a solitary 'hmm.'

'So, Stuart,' I repeat.

She is smiling at Stuart, who is running his hands over her thighs.

'Oh,' she says.

'Is that all you can say?' I can see she is struggling to talk. She does not want this conversation. Stuart is taking priority; for me, that says it all.

'Okay, yeah, okay…' she says. 'Look, I can't talk right now, the security man's coming over.'

I know it's an excuse to get rid of me. 'Okay, see you, we can talk later.'

'Bye,' she says, without averting her gaze from Stuart.

Putting the phone away, I peer around the door and she is whispering in Stuart's ear. What is being said is indecipherable, but it must be highly amusing because both of them start laughing. I have to assume it's a joke at my expense. Perhaps she was telling him she is now a free agent, free to give him her undivided attention?

Amanda is writing something on her pad. Not a short note, something longer. Perhaps a letter to Stuart, telling him they are finished? It was good while it lasted, but now it's over, and she wants to take up with someone more experienced. Someone like me.

I toy with the idea of walking in on them, to shock her; confront them both while they are naked on the bed.

Someone dropping a pen returns me to reality. Amanda looks concerned.

'You okay?' she mouths, after seeing an evidently sad expression on my face.

'I'm alright,' I mouth in return. 'Tell you later.'

She nods in agreement, then returns her attention to the meeting. Everyone is still trying to be attentive, but I bet they all wish they were somewhere else. Not long now, though. It will soon be the Easter weekend.

I have a more subtle plan, a plan which will tell the whole world about her and Stuart. I make my way to the study, where I pull a briefcase out of the filing cabinet. Inside are three smoke canisters, a borrowed idea from a spy story I read recently, each of them cleverly disguised as common aerosols: furniture polish, shaving foam and antiperspirant. In the book, these provided an effective smoke screen, handy cover in difficult situations when the agent needed a quick means of escape. They provide the impression that a fire is raging, but once used are almost impossible to detect. Perfect.

Systematically priming and placing each of the canisters in position, I have only seconds in which to make my escape. 'Furniture polish' inside the kitchen; 'shaving foam' next to the door leading to the bathroom; and 'antiperspirant' just inside the door of the main bedroom, carefully placed so as not to be seen by Stuart and Amanda, though they are still too engrossed to notice me.

Soon, a thick fog develops. One final look into the bedroom and Stuart is standing beside the bed, while Amanda is lying in ecstasy. On leaving the flat, all I can hear are Amanda's shrieks of pleasure and Stuart's grunts.

An ear-piercing alarm reverberates around the landing and stairs, as I join other residents leaving the building. I am one of the first out, and instead of following the others to the official congregational point on the far side of the car park, I turn sharply left and make for a small crop of trees running alongside the building. Waiting amongst the bushes, I reach into my jacket and pull out a packet of cigarettes, one of which I light.

The fire engines appear, but the shouts and jeers from the crowd are louder than any of their sirens.

Looking across to the main entrance, I see Amanda and Stuart racing through the door, both completely naked. The smoke in the flat would have been too dense for them to have the time or vision to find their clothes.

Stuart is red faced with embarrassment; Amanda is screaming obscenities, not at the mocking crowd, but at herself. On reaching the outside, the first thing she sees are people reaching for their phones, so they can capture the spectacle. She must know the pictures and videos will go viral, and to make matters worse, the firemen seem to be having trouble finding blankets for her and Stuart to cover their modesty.

Amanda is obviously wondering why there is a smile on my face. I look over to Stuart; he is doodling on his pad, totally oblivious to both Amanda and the meeting. Candice is winding up. Not long now before we can all escape. Amanda is doing her piece, thanking all those who have spoken, and everyone who has attended (honestly, we deserve a medal). Rupert thanks Amanda for organising the meeting and suggests a round of applause, in recognition of her efforts. The clapping dies and people eagerly pack their things ready for a hasty exit. Most appear relieved as we file out.

As I tag along at the end, Amanda calls me over.

'What was the joke? I could see you smiling,' she asks.

'Oh, nothing really,' I reply.

'Go on, I won't tell anyone else.'

Since we are alone, I decide this is as good a time as any to ask her about the rumours. 'What's all this I hear about Rupert and Fiona?' I pause for dramatic effect. 'And about you having an affair in retribution?'

'Oh, don't believe a word. Nothing could be further from the truth.'

'I couldn't help noticing the eye contact between you and Stuart. For me, that said it all. It's Stuart you are seeing, right? Don't worry, I'll keep it a secret; keep everyone guessing.'

'Oh, that,' she said, waving the thought away. 'We occasionally flirt, you know what I'm like, and he is cute, isn't he? I wouldn't say no—'

'Once upon a time you wouldn't have had second thoughts.'

A rare bashfulness comes over her. 'Yes…but I'm too old for all that now.'

Her coyness is unconvincing; she would never let a chance like Stuart go by as easily as that. But still, who am I to argue? Though I am still determined to get to the bottom of the rumours, there must be some truth in them, somewhere.

'I do have some gossip though, but you have to keep this to yourself. It mustn't become common knowledge.'

'Mum's the word,' I reply.

'Rupert's not seeing Fiona, and I'm not seeing Stuart. It's Fiona who is seeing Stuart. Now, you know the rules concerning office romances, they could get into big trouble. That's why I've promised to keep it a secret.'

'Rupert's not having an affair?'

'He wouldn't dare,' laughs Amanda. 'Well, he can, but he wouldn't dare leave me. I made sure of that when I drew up the prenup, remember? If he did leave, I would get half of everything, including half of his earnings for the next five years. I am not going to be left penniless like his first wife. And you know what I'm like where it comes to money.'

'Don't I remember! When we shared the flat in Camden you would go through the bills with a fine toothcomb; make sure we never went short.'

'The house is worth nearly ten million, so that'll be five million, and I've roughly worked out that with all his shares, business interests and directorships, as well as this place, I'll get about twelve hundred thousand a year. If he leaves me, of course.'

I knew Rupert earnt a tidy sum, but never in my wildest dreams did I imagine it would be well over two million a year. 'Wow,' I said, with a broad grin.

'Don't forget the flat in Archway. That's worth a packet too.'

'Oh yes, how can I forget the flat?' I replied, thinking of the daydream. I beamed, but there was no way I was going to tell her about my imagined humiliations of her and Stuart.

'So, anyway. What I was going to say was that Rupert's going away for a few days. How would you like to come over? I can show you the new extension, give you a guided tour, and we can reminisce over old times. The pool's just been cleaned, and it would be waste to see it neglected.' She winked 'And besides, Rupert's wine cellar is long overdue a visit.'

Sweet Dreams

Some nights, the dreams were genial; cheerful; enough to lift his broken spirit. Other nights they proved malevolent; sometimes surreal; obscure to the point of having no meaning at all.

Tonight's began with him commanding a small fleet of destroyers. He had already lost two vessels and was determined not to lose a third. They were being held in a state of fear and awe, at the sight of two colossal female figures, more like statues, locked in combat in the middle of the ocean. Shouting down the radio, he ordered the other vessels to hold back; to not get any closer. The figures could not go on forever, one would have to win at some point; only then would they be able to get away.

The fact was, no matter how hard they tried, they could not escape. Both at least one hundred, if not two hundred, feet tall, it was the shorter of the two who was winning the battle. Several times, she managed to knock her taller opponent into the water. But every time, her opponent managed to regain her feet. That was the reason why they could not get away. The continual collapsing and rising of the taller figure was creating massive vortexes, causing the vessels to be sucked back into the line of battle and almost certain destruction.

The destroyers had tried firing at them: torpedoes and heavy artillery. But all to no effect. It was no use wasting any more ammunition, the figures were invincible. Each giant appeared to be made of stone. Yet this was merely a hard, outer shell, encasing a raging inferno. The sailors covered their faces as the taller one's case split, spilling out smoke and flame. Their hands, too, were a mass of flame, threatening the survival of the ships as they sprayed huge swathes of blistering fire in all directions.

It was a hopeless situation. The vast plumes of flame were burning his fleet to a cinder, and he could only watch as the third ship was about to succumb to the violent firestorm. It was useless trying to look for survivors; the only mercy of this situation was instant incineration, and if by some miracle some did survive, they would almost certainly perish in the boiling sea around them.

The two combatants seemed to be slowing. Perhaps they were tiring? At last! The Commander saw his chance.

'Retreat! Retreat!' he hollered, as the sea calmed. There was relief all round. At last, they could escape. Though they could not save the others, they could at least save themselves.

'Quick, full reverse, then hard port!' the Commander screamed into the mouthpiece. Almost immediately he felt the engines grinding to a halt in preparation for the about turn. Too late: the females had resumed their battle, this time with even greater ferocity. He was concentrating on the instruments when, suddenly, there was a blinding flash. Stunned into immobility, he could only watch as molten flame engulfed his bridge. His movement returning, he went to grab the handrail alongside him, only to stare in horror as the flesh on his hands melted into the hot metal rail.

A meaningless void. He stood in emptiness. No walls, no ceiling, no floor. Just whiteness, all around. He turned, first his head, then his body. Continuously turning, he looked about him, searching…for something…anything. Three hundred and sixty degrees he turned, finding nothing except empty whiteness.

Suddenly, he swivelled his head. He thought he had seen something. His trained eyes were sharp; even the slightest detail he was certain to notice. He readjusted his eyes to focus. Yes, there it was: a dark speck, just visible in the distance. He would have missed it had he not caught the darkness in the corner of his eye. He could not see what it was, not from this distance, so he decided to go and take a look. It could be another person, then at least he would not be alone; they might be able to explain this white desert to him, and why he is here. Alternatively, it could be a mirage, similar to those experienced in normal deserts. Anything was possible.

He could not wait to reach the dark speck. He must have been walking for half an hour, an hour? If he had his watch, he would know. But he did not. Indeed, he had no idea what had happened to it. He was sure it had been on his wrist earlier, whenever, and wherever earlier had been. Shame, it was his best watch too. The one Alicia had bought for him. Yes, Alicia had given it to him, he remembered that. But, once again, he could not quite remember when that had been. A special occasion, perhaps? Yes, that was right, a special occasion…

He dwelt on the thought of what special occasion it had been. Never mind the time: he did not even know what day it was, or the date, or year. Looking down, he saw that he was wearing clothes he had not worn for years: green chinos and a green polo shirt. Clothes he thought he had discarded long ago. The situation was getting stranger by the minute.

The dark speck was taking form. He squinted. The figure looked like…Emerald? Emerald? He had not seen her since…there was a vague memory of them deciding to stop seeing each other, but that had been…when, exactly? His memory was a haze and the details a blur.

The time it took him to reach her gave him a chance to think. That was right, the affair had lasted for some time; there had been the torment of having to choose between her and Alicia…Alicia? Emerald? Emerald…Alicia? Emerald was the exact opposite of Alicia. Short, with dark plaited hair, in harmony with her unblemished, ebony complexion. And still with that sensuous stare. He was in love with her all over again.

As ever, she was provocatively dressed, wearing clothes he had never seen before, or at least, could not remember having seen: dark, ripped jeans and a black, cropped top, zip sufficiently undone to reveal a tantalising glimpse of her taut bosom. She was still as beautiful as she always had been and gave off an aura of eroticism which reminded him of their hours of heated passion. He was definitely in love again.

He had meant to ask where he was but seeing her after all this time threw him.

'Hello, where have you been?' she demanded, as he stepped closer.

He mustered some form of answer. 'I was going to ask you the same,' he murmured. 'You haven't changed, at least, not since I last saw you.' He searched his mind. 'How long ago was that, exactly?'

'We are both here, that's what's important,' she replied, mysteriously. 'Come on,' she continued, while walking away from him. Her voice still rang with authority, and her walk was confident and self-assured. Where she led, others always followed.

'Where to?'

She stopped and turned back to him, answering sarcastically. 'Where to? As if you need to ask. Do I have to explain everything?' Undoing the top button of her jeans, she eased them open. 'We've got a lot of catching up to do, have we not?' she continued seductively, sliding a finger into the dark hole she had just revealed.

They were playing hide and seek in and around a clean, pristine, Georgian style mansion; using it as a playground, taking it in turns to cover their eyes and count to a five hundred, while the other ran off to find a place to hide. They spent hours there, exploring every room in the house: the upstairs and downstairs drawing rooms, the dining room, the kitchens, the multitude of bedrooms, even the scullery. Each time, the seeker was rewarded with a kiss, and passionate intimacy. Ah yes, their intimacy. How he remembered their intimacy.

They were good together; their love making was perfection. Better now? Perhaps. It was difficult to tell, it had been such a long time…but they were together again now, that was the important thing. As one again, as it should be, as it should always have been?

He was lost. He had made his way to the servant's quarters, at the top of the house, could not for the life of him remember the way back. He could only hope that Emerald would find him. He had tried to find his own way back, but there appeared to be so many different routes; whichever way he decided to go, she was sure to be using another. He was better off staying where he was, she would turn up eventually.

Waiting for her to arrive, he elected to explore the various rooms in the attic. At least it would pass the time. The first room he entered was a bedroom. There was a single bed, a small chest of drawers and a wardrobe. This must be a room used by one of the single members of staff: a young footman or chambermaid, perhaps? There were three more rooms with a similar layout, then a larger one. This has a double bed and much larger pieces of furniture, so was most probably used by a senior, married couple. He noticed that there were no personal effects in any of the rooms and, as with the downstairs, everything was brand new. It was as if the whole house were waiting to be used, by people he was yet to meet, or never would.

There was also a nursery, presumably used by the children of the house, with a rocking horse sitting in the corner. As a child, he had spent hours playing on one similar. Sitting on the white leather saddle, childhood memories came flooding back: pre-school, when he had been looked after by the family nanny; school, and the years of being bullied…the latter years were too sad to ponder, so he decided to train his thoughts elsewhere.

The horse was clearly made for a youngster but was large enough for him to sit on. What seemed like only minutes passed, except, from the changing angle of the sun, as it shone through a skylight, it was obvious he had been there for much longer. Emerald…where was she? She should have found him by now. Perhaps she had and was playing a game: he half expected her to pop her head around the door any second, saying 'fooled you!'

He waited, and waited, and waited. Any longer and he would have to assume she had given up looking for him; gone away forever, never to return. There may have been perpetual daylight outside, but a darkness was forming in his heart, and would continue to form until Emerald reappeared. Trying to avoid the inner shadows, he directed his mind elsewhere. The sunshine only highlighted the fact that everything in the house was white. He should probably have noticed it before but had been too engrossed in their game to pay attention. He was paying attention now.

The rocking horse was white. All the toys were white. The nursery was painted white, and so was every room he had been in: the walls, the doors, the ceilings, the floors and all the furnishings. Everything, including the pictures on the walls, which had a white hue to their scenes.

The only thing that was not white was the steak meal he was suddenly eating, and the ruby red wine he was about to pour into his and Emerald's glasses. A toast, celebrating Emerald's new promotion, happy times, yes, happy times.

'Trust you to be clumsy,' she giggled, watching him miss his mouth and tip almost a full glass of red wine down his white dinner jacket.

'You're just as bad,' he laughed, as Emerald took a bite of her enormous burger, sending red ketchup down the front of her white top.

'It was you who insisted we came for a burger,' she fumed. 'I was just as happy with a pizza, but no, we had to leave before they brought our order over.'

'Well, you were flirting with the chap who took the order. I could see your eyes scanning him as he went back to the counter. I could guess what was going through your mind.'

'Well? And what were you just doing? Oh, yeah, that's right. Chatting up the girl behind the counter. You would have asked her out if I hadn't butted in with what I wanted.'

'I'm as bad as you, then.'

She looked around the crowded burger restaurant to see if anyone else was close enough to hear. They had not yet drawn attention to themselves, and she wanted to keep it that way. She leant forward to whisper. 'Yes, but at least the lad at the pizza place was cute; much better looking than yours.'

'Okay, okay. We're even now,' he replied, trying to avoid a scene. He knew full well how their arguments usually went. They always got heated, blowing the original issue well out of proportion. 'But what are we going to do about that ketchup?' he continued, changing the subject. 'Want me to get a cloth or something, some napkins perhaps?'

'Do what you like,' she snapped, causing even more ketchup to spill from the burger. 'I don't bloody care,' she glared, looking down at the even larger red stain on her top.

'Red…okay…the red medical ones are never meant to leave the office, correct?' asked Emerald, holding up a red folder.

'That's right,' he replied, blushing.

'So, why were they in your case?'

'I was taking them home to look through. Anyway, what were you doing going through my case?'

She paused for a moment as she put the folders back where she had found them. 'I thought there were no secrets between us, don't you trust me?'

'Course I trust you, but I am the chief, and this is a department case.'

'That's no answer—'

He was going to continue, but she stopped him with a kiss on the lips. She smiled. 'I was only teasing. Of course I know you take papers home. I don't mind. Honest. I know I can trust you not to lose them.'

'That's alright then, you had me a worried for a moment there.'

She laughed. 'I know. Your face was a picture! Anyway, I can see why you come into these woods, they are so peaceful.'

'They are a good escape. You can lose yourself for hours, not in the literal sense, of course, just metaphorically. Besides, I need places to relax.'

'Like this spot, it's so secluded.'

'Exactly. I can sit here for hours and contemplate things.'

'Like those red files?'

'Like those red files. There's never anyone around, so I can read them in peace.'

'What, no one? Not even a freak, hungry for sex?' she teased. 'You should be careful, a fit young man like yourself, all alone.' She paused. 'Easy prey.'

'I haven't had the luxury of meeting one yet,' he laughed.

'You have,' she laughed back. 'Me! I'm a sex freak, and I simply can't get enough of you. Never have, ever since I joined the department.'

'Yeah, sex mad,' he laughed back. 'That's why I come here, to escape.'

'I can imagine this place gets quite popular with courting couples, it's so private. I'd be my element here. Anyway, since I'm your boss, it's my duty to make you work. Ever done it in the open?'

'Are you sure no one knows you booked this hotel,' she asked, surveying the basic furnishings. 'You know, there are no secrets in the department. You have heard the rumours about us, right?'

'I booked it in my friend's name, don't worry. No one will find out.'

'You had better be sure of that.'

'Trust me.'

'Course I do, how long have we got?'

'I'd say another hour, and then we had better get back to the office.'

He pressed his lips against hers, and she responded, and for several minutes they stayed there, locked in a deep kiss.

The feel of Emerald's tender lips against his mouth, the sensation of holding her in his unhindered, strong, healthy arms suddenly dissipated into Alicia, shaking him.

'Get off, you silly old fool! That's the third time this week I've woken up to find you kissing me. Whatever have you been dreaming about?'

He was startled. Being awakened in the middle of the night was a shock in itself, but now having to quickly find something constructive to say was torture.

'I was dreaming about when we first got together, remember?' That would do, he dared not mention Emerald. Even though she had found out about Emerald long ago, and all had been forgiven, she still got upset at the mention of her name.

Her face tightened as she stared at him. 'Of course, I do! I'll never forget. I will always remember it as if it were yesterday. We've had some good times together, haven't we?'

'And some of it will forever be nothing more than a dream now.'

'You can say that again,' she responded, pecking him on the lips.

He smiled. 'You will look after me, won't you?'

'You're being silly now, course I will.'

'That's good. We've always looked out for each other, haven't we?'

She sensed fear and nervousness in his voice. 'You're getting emotional again, stop it. As we have always said, I'm here for you and you're here for me. Now, try and get some sleep. You've got a big day tomorrow.'

'Yes, I hope it goes well.'

'Course it will. Remember, the stroke specialist was more than happy with you the last time. And you can tell him that you've managed to get to the other side of the room all by yourself. Now, that's an enormous improvement, isn't it?'

'It is. I'm getting a lot better.'

She rested her tired head on the pillow. She might have only been fifty-two, but she looked much older. The months spent looking after him were taking their toll. But that didn't matter, they had been together for many years, and she had vowed never to give up on him. 'There we go, see? Things are improving. And you're in safe hands,' she continued reassuringly. 'Don't worry, you'll never be alone. Let's talk about this in the morning, hmm? It's time to go back to sleep, our days of staying awake all night are long behind us.'

'You're right,' he agreed, remembering their once active love life. 'We're both too old for all that now,' he added, snuggling down under the bedclothes. Then, with a disjointed smile on his contorted face, he whispered, 'Night, Alicia. Love you.'

'Night, night, darling. Love you too. Sweet dreams.'

BV - #0081 - 080221 - C0 - 197/132/18 - PB - 9781912964611